MAHIHKAN LAKE

OTHER BOOKS BY R.P. MACINTYRE

Apart (Groundwood Books, 2007)

Feeding at Nine (Thistledown Press, 2006)

Revved (Thistledown Press, 2002)

The Crying Jesus (Thistledown Press, 1997)

The Blue Camaro (Thistledown Press, 1994)

Yuletide Blues (Thistledoiwn Press, 1991)

MAHIHKAN LAKE

R. P. MacIntyre

thistledown press

Thistledown Press Ltd.
410 2nd Avenue North
Saskatoon, Saskatchewan, S7K 2C3
www.thistledownpress.com

Library and Archives Canada Cataloguing in Publication
MacIntyre, R. P. (Roderick Peter), 1947-, author
Mahihkan Lake / R.P. MacIntyre.
Issued in print and electronic formats.
ISBN 978-1-77187-053-5 (paperback).–ISBN 978-1-77187-086-3 (html).–
ISBN 978-1-77187-087-0 (pdf)
I. Title.
PS8575.I67M35 2015   C813'.54   C2015-905165-7
C2015-905166-5

Cover and book design by Jackie Forrie
Printed and bound in Canada

Canada Council   Conseil des Arts
for the Arts   du Canada

Canadä

Thistledown Press gratefully acknowledges the financial assistance of the Canada Council for the Arts, the Saskatchewan Arts Board, and the Government of Canada for its publishing program.

Acknowledgments

Writing a novel is like a high-diving act; you jump off the tower and hope there's water in that little tiny pool at the bottom. Fortunately, there's lots of water in mine.

First and foremost, I need to thank my partner and patron of forty-odd years, Sharyn Swann, without whom not much of this could ever have happened and to whom I am forever indebted. The Wild Rice Writers' Group kept my nose to the grindstone for twelve years in La Ronge. The Saskatchewan Arts Board pitched in with financial subsistence for one of those years. Susan Dormer and Suzanne McNab provided early feedback. Her Honour Felicia Daunt advised in legal matters that are part of this story; fellow biker David Smith advised in matters of commercial trucking. Finally, my long-suffering editor, Harriet Richards, who always manages to make this process as painless as possible and makes me look better than I really am. Thank you all at Thistledown Press. It's hard to believe it's been twenty-four years.

My childhood friends,
Chuck Carriere and Jerry Knorr.

If I were to live another life, I would take more care with gasoline and avoid high speeds mixed with gin. I would thank Denny for being my tongue. I would apologize to Dianne because nothing is as it seems. We are born squalling in the company of strangers. Sometimes we get to know them, sometimes not. We learn to walk and maybe to ride a Road King and fix it if our hands do what they are told; we learn that the sun will rise even though we live half our life in shadows or darkness; we take what we are given, more or less, run with it as best we can, and then die. If we are lucky, we die close to home or trying to get there, like me. Others, even your brother, will assume what they will. And that poor idiot trucker will get the blame. My fault, though.

Now, my brother and sister are looking to find a place for me in their lives. I'm curious to find out where that will be. I'm curious to find out what secrets they will hide and which ones they will show since they are extremely self-centred and don't really have a clue about me, or about themselves for that matter.

Life is just full of surprises They would be surprised by my words here. They thought that because I could not speak fluently that I could not think as well. I suppose it's a natural enough assumption -- nothing is as it seems. So while I miss the wind in my face, I am quite happy to be dead."

Dave Mackenzie-Givens 1955 – 2005

Blue

1

I knew it was Dave. You could hear him a half mile away. Straight pipes barking from his gleaming midnight Road King, all 1,600 cubic centimetres tucked into the chromed-out Twin Cam 96 V-twin that he would have re-bored himself. Only weekend warriors like lawyers and dentists, all decked out in their badass blacks, only these rode stock. Or worse, Buells.

The percussive roar grew louder the closer it got, suddenly easing into its *potato-potato* murmur till it ceased altogether. A moment of silence. Then the unmistakable heft of Dave's steel-toed, thick-soled boots striking the risers as he climbed above the paint shop to my apartment where my nominal rent is subsidized by my nominal job as night watchman for the store below — to which I do not even have a key. This casts a shadow over the efficacy of my role if someone should ever try to steal a gallon of latex primer at two in the morning. Except if it was Dave; I could tell by his footsteps.

Dave banged on the door. He did not wait for me to answer, not that I was going to get up for him anyway. I'm too fat and too lazy. I buttoned my shirt, though, and tried to comb what's left of my hair back into place with my fingertips. I don't want to look like a complete slob even though that's what I am. I was already into a warm buzz, having started with the hair of the dog a couple hours earlier. It was about noon. No need to waste time.

Dave entered, a big man, and closed the door like a bear swatting at flies. Dave always made big entrances.

"Fuf-fuf-fuck it's cold," he said.

"It's not snowing." I steadied my gin.

"It's fuf-ucking m-m . . . " and here Dave's throat and jaw seized up as it often did on "m"s, " . . . mid-July," he finished.

I resisted the urge to complete Dave's sentence. I didn't always.

"You sis-till drinking that shit?"

It was a rhetorical question. He didn't expect an answer. I shrugged instead. The less said to Dave, the better. If you talked, he had to answer. Talking was not his strong suit.

Dave yanked a bandana from his head. His hair sprang into shape like a copper Brillo pad — except now it was flecked with grey. He used the bandana to wipe his nose, a habit of his because of its super-sensitivity, and he was conscious that it might be runny. The burn and ensuing mediocre surgery had mottled his face to an uncertain texture that flared red from time to time. His mouth was still perfect though, the lips of a Cree or Highland warrior from somewhere in his mongrel past. He surveyed my apartment.

"Got any mmmore?"

"Help yourself," I pointed to the fridge. "In the freezer."

Dave strode to it, his boots *kalumping* across the floor. I wondered if the paint salesmen below were concerned for their safety — that their ceiling might collapse. Dave's heft was mostly muscle. He took the bottle from the freezer and carried it like a club. He didn't look for a glass but returned to sit on a stool across from me, straddling it like a bike. It's where I sat when I practiced the guitar — not too often these days. I'm better at growing my fingernails. Have my right hand — my pick'n hand — honed like a raven's claws.

Dave was in a power position — forcing me to lift my chin from my chest. This would be important. Dave wanted something I was not going to say no to. He unscrewed the top of the Bombay, took a swig, then reached into his jacket and pulled out an envelope. He began to pass it to me but snatched it back just as I reached for it. I left my hand hanging mid-air.

"D-don't r-read it. D-don't open it. D-don't *nnothing* it." He then placed it on my waiting fingers. On it, penned in Dave's hieroglyphic scrawl, was *Dianne.*

"Gggive it to Didi," he said, choking on the "g". However, he had no trouble articulating the redundant "d's" when he referred to our sister.

"Why don't you give it to her?"

"Cccan't," he said.

I knew there was no point in asking why he couldn't do it himself, that he probably saw Dianne about as often as I did, which was almost never. Maybe our mom would die — which she was bound to do in the next four or five years — and we'd see her at the funeral. I could give it to her then. So could Dave, for that matter, except Dave would not be going to Mom's funeral — not if she was the second last person on the planet. He'd let her lie there and rot to die alone. I wouldn't blame him. But really, the opportunities to see Dianne were few and far between. We might as well live on different planets.

Having completed his task, Dave then stood and made a kind of flourish out of screwing the top back onto the gin — my gin. "I'll t-take this," he said holding up the bottle. He headed back to the door.

"Where are you going?" I had hoped he'd settle in for a bit and maybe we'd have a visit.

"M-m-Mahihkan," he said.

Dave'd been staying there, at the cabin on the lake. I knew that. I watched his big, grizzly back shuffle out the door, then listened as he clumped back down the stairs. I had the kettle on to steam open the letter before his bike roared off.

That was the last time I saw him.

The note read, "Sorry for what happened in Kelowna and everything else. Jimmy Matheson contacted me. He wants to meet you. D."

It's harder to reseal an envelope than it is to seal it.

❧

I am not a violent man; I don't like violence — can't stand "ultimate fighting" or whatever they call it — and I avoid contact with whatever violence seems to be happening nearby — car accidents, for example. I cross the street. Take a detour. Violence is fraught with pain, and I think not getting involved with pain is a good policy. Pain hurts.

Despite that, I can't get over how much violence and pain has been in my life. My mother used to beat Dave daily; I had an uncle and a cousin (not to mention a brother) die in motorcycle accidents; an aunt committed suicide; my dad drowned in his own phlegm (I doubt that you can get more violent than that). Violence seems to be pretty much all around me. You can't turn on a TV without seeing something on fire or blow up. Why I don't own a TV. Why I cross the street.

Why I make music.

All I've ever wanted to do is make music. And maybe drink a bit. Trouble is, I could never do it alone — make music, that is. I'm very accomplished at solitary drinking.

Rolling Stone Magazine once said Rick and I were "aspiring for the same league as Simon and Garfunkel." But then, who wasn't? Still, even a mention in those days meant a lot for a couple of Canadian kids trying to make a living in the Maritimes. We called ourselves Icegate. It was just after Watergate and we thought if it had happened in Canada, it would have been Icegate. We also thought it was pretty darn funny and clever. It worked for us for two years. Then Ricky and our manager got smucked at a level crossing on their way back from a party in Truro that I was too drunk to attend. It was about a week after *Hiding* went gold. The LP is now a collector's item but I don't even own a copy. We had simpatico, Rick and I, but I don't even think about it anymore. What's the point? I tried gigging solo for a few years, but I wasn't any good at it. Not really. It wasn't the same after the night fell. Although my metaphorical *night* didn't actually *fall* — as though onto its face — it did stumble around, however, lost in a kind of shadowy dark place that looked a lot like the sun was on the other side of the planet. All that's left now from my sunny youth is the hardware — amps, speakers, mixers and two or three boxes of shit that might have plugged into something or other at one time but have no possible use whatsoever now, including an Ampex 1250 reel-to-reel that was top-of-the-line forty years ago, early solid-state mixed with vacuum-tubes for God's sake. I suppose that makes it priceless now as I hear some of this gear is making a comeback for that warm, honey-thick sound that digital just can't duplicate.

This was the equipment I used when *Hiding* was big. The full title was actually *Hiding in a Sheepskin Glove*. It didn't make any sense but it had that sinister "Hotel California" feel — *he's hiding, hiding, hiding in a sheepskin glove* — sort of thing. I based it on a story from my long-dead grandmother Dupuis, a pinch-mouthed woman who always looked terrified. Or maybe just startled. But when she told that story, it made your hair stand up. It made you feel like prey. Like the wolf was outside the door.

It made you feel like Dave was around.

If Dave hadn't given me the damned note or letter (or whatever it was) that I was supposed to give to Dianne, scrawled on the back of a blank, grease-stained service invoice, none of this would have happened. Dave would have picked his fight with the side draft, lost, got tangled under the truck, bounced around like a bloody paper cup, and that would have been that. Game over. I would have continued drinking myself into blissful oblivion none the wiser, even though I'm fully aware that wisdom is a tolerable virtue, despite its aspirations, and that once you have it, there's not much you can do about it, except maybe deny, deny, deny.

But all that does is call attention. And God knows I don't want to call attention. I have all the attention I can handle and then some. But I promise myself I'll start drinking again when I turn seventy-five, if I should live that long.

It's only another twenty-five years. I wonder if it will be a happy or a sad event. It will be an event though — starting anything is an event.

I remember when I started to drink, the event — my first *drunk*. Four boys — we may have been fifteen — one forty-ounce bottle of rye whiskey, one night and one tent in the middle of a cow pasture. We drank till we grew blurred and leaden, then toppled over one-by-one into dismembered heaps, our mouths open, drool trickling down our pink jowls — a sty full of demented hogs. Eventually, the urge to relieve myself grew pressing, as did the stink of daylight, and I crawled out into the morning sun, its lightening whiteness hammering both inside and outside my skull, and plunged my right hand wrist-deep into a fresh cow pie. I then barfed over the rest of my arm. THAT was an event. You'd think it would be an end to drinking, and although rye whiskey and I never kept much company after that, it was just a start. The process of quitting took a bit longer. Somewhere over thirty years. And I'm not done yet.

Just about everything's a process — life, death, you name it. Some are natural — like what shape your nose grows into or when your teeth start falling out — but most are learned, and for every class of folk — a different process set.

For example, there is a certain class of people who know exactly how to use the four knobs on an Ampex 1250, just as there is a certain class that know the exact order of all Twelve Steps in the program; combined, they make the alcoholic-musician class — my class. There is another class familiar with arranging for bail, or failing that, navigating through visitors' protocol at a Federal

Corrections Facility. Neither of these things are remotely like anything you see on TV. The smell of institutional waiting rooms, the tediousness of forms in triplicate, the disinterestedness of people in uniforms and how they never make eye contact — except when they are assessing you, the sparse coldness of it all. I can thank Dave for these arcane bits of knowledge — Dave and his missing fingerprints.

Nobody ever called him David. David was a sissy name, and he was no sissy. He was hard-boiled biker — an outlaw — also a very fine mechanic. Only our mother persisted in calling him David, and only because she knew he hated it.

We were raised like brothers and I never thought of him as otherwise even though we were not actual flesh and blood. Dave was a foster kid , a year older than me, and arrived when I was about three. Dave, however, peed his bed and stuttered so intensely that he was a virtual mute. I did his talking for him. Mom beat Dave for no reason that I could see. She seldom touched me. But Davey was always black and blue.

We shared a room. At first, we shared a bed as well, till our dad installed bunks. Dave made me sleep on the top bunk, not because he was afraid of peeing on me, but because his frantic twisting and writhing away from his midnight demons threw him right out of bed some nights. He knew he'd do the same on the upper bunk and didn't want to fall that far. "You sa-sa-sa sleep up there," he stammered, as though it was a kind of banishment. But we both knew it was a privilege, that the older brother always slept on the top bunk — even if he wasn't really your brother.

Every other Saturday, my dad would take me to Bill's Barbershop where my hair was cut by a gentle old man who smelled of spearmint chewing gum and barber's talc and whose name, I assumed, was Bill. With his strong, soft hands, he would set me in the great nickel-coated throne, upholstered in red leather, and let me help pump it up as high as it would go. "Just a trim, or some off the top too?" he would ask Dad, then talk about how Chevs were a piece of junk, and why Gordie Howe was maybe the greatest player ever, and why Dief the Chief should be "taken out to the alley and given a haircut down to his shoulders." Even though I could imagine that this would be a very messy haircut, right out behind Bill's shop with lots of blood and a head rolling around in the back alley, I knew it was a joke about Dief the Chief — whoever he was — intended for everyone in the shop to laugh at — which they did. It was always such an adult pleasure on those Saturdays, and part of getting ready for Sunday mass — to be neat and tidy for God.

It never occurred to me that Davey was not part of this bi-weekly ritual, that instead, Mom cropped his hair short to his skull with an old pair of hand clippers. On those rare occasions they were used on me — in emergencies — the clippers hooked and pulled, and made tears come to my eyes even though I knew I shouldn't cry, that my mom would be mad if I cried. The opposite was true for Davey; Mom got mad when he *didn't* cry, and Davey *never* cried. This probably caused him more bruises than anything.

I assumed that Davey was different for certain things, like it was okay for him to get beaten for no reason and to have a stutter and to want to sleep on the lower bunk. Perhaps I even thought that was why our penises were different. I did not realize then that I was circumcised and David was not. When you are five or six-years old, you accept most things as they are. It does not occur to you that they should be different, that they could be different. Everything is in the moment, the present tense. A child's mind.

Early memories: I liked some things. Disliked others. Yes or no. Black or white, reacting to the fullest. Nothing is ever halfway. I frown at soggy green cabbage that Mommy boils and boils. She does this to stink up the kitchen. Serves it with fried liver. Each swallow fights its bitter way down. I eat it, though. And throw up. I look at Davey. He sniggers. Peels open the top of his pocket. A purple-grey chuck of liver peeks at me. He gets slapped. Sent to his room. Our room. I think it would be better to be slapped and sent to our room than to have to be good and eat the liver and throw up.

Another time.

Daddy's cigarette smoke burns my eyes. He coughs so hard I think his guts will spill out. I hide his cigarettes. Davey gets accused of stealing them. Davey gets beaten, again. He looks at me with his cool-blue eyes with a hint of a smile in them. He knows. And he knows it's pointless to say anything. I am silent through this, even though I know too. I'll never hide my dad's cigarettes again. I give them to Davey. He'll know what to do.

He does, too — he smokes them. He is ten.

Dianne had arrived by then and was old enough to know that smoking is a dangerous and bad thing or else why would we be hiding behind the garage where Davey smoked and we watched, too scared to join. Dianne took great glee at the smoke rings drifting like chain links from

Davey's mouth. She would jump and try to grab them. Where did Davey learn to do that?

Occasionally in our room, Davey would sit on his bunk, rocking back and forth. Sometimes the rocking grew severe and he would bang his head against the wall or the edge of the bed. I would let him do it for a while because I knew it calmed him somehow. But then, before it actually hurt him — and he could do this till he bled — I would say, "Davey, don't." And he would stop. He would look at me with those eyes and he would stop.

But it was not all like this. Not always. Not at Mahihkan Lake.

At the lake, our dad had built a small cabin where we spent our Julys and sometimes part of August. Mom and Dad bought the small lot upon which the cabin sat, two hundred feet from shorefront, for five-thousand dollars back when there was barely a gravel-top road skidding through the bush. Here, Dave was different — wilder, freer. More than once he'd stripped completely naked and raced into the water at midday, giggling, oblivious of nervous neighbours. I dutifully waded out into the water carrying his trunks, then dogpaddled to the big black rock that sat sentinel twenty feet beyond. I'd make him put them on before coming back ashore.

Dave stuttered less at the lake — some days not at all. Something in the full, clean air, or the black water lapping on the purple sand, or the damp cool of night, or the loons echoing off the rocks and jack pine made a difference for him, for at least one month out of twelve.

Dave barely finished grade ten. School was not his friend. He stopped going mid-May on his sixteenth birthday, when he dug a hole in the backyard, filled it with his school books, and set them afire. The same day, he moved into the garage although he still used the bathroom in the basement of the house.

The garage, like many in our neighbourhood, was not used as a place to store a car even though that was its intended purpose. It was used instead as a large storage bin for anything that Mom did not want in the house — mostly old furniture that she did not want to throw out. This was perfect for Dave who organized it all and split the space in two with a thick, black curtain: On one side was his shop where he worked on bikes and just about anything else that required a wrench or blowtorch. On the other — *The Inferno,* his name for it — he created a cozy little black-walled den full of rock 'n roll records, speakers, stereo, posters, ashtrays, a fridge, a bed, and an assortment of milk crates in various configurations, plus the various bits of furniture than Mom had discarded and that Dave found tolerable.

It was in the garage, while twisting Harley bolts and listening to rock 'n roll, that he grew his hair. Long, thick, red, and shiny. Girls lusted after his hair. He wasn't good with them, however. He got tongue-tied and would stutter helplessly in their company. So he just kept his mouth shut. This made him all the more attractive. Girls would gather and talk to him for hours while he would wrench away at whatever was handy, stinking of tobacco and WD-40. They thought he was such a good listener.

Dave lived there till he went to the hospital. I hung around pretending to practise the guitar, but really it was so I could attempt to meet some of those girls who flitted like the butterflies around Mom's cabbage — not that there was anything remotely cabbagey about Dave. If he was a food, it was steak. Rare.

I failed though, with the girls, just as I have continued to fail with women all my life. Back then, it was my thin, stringy hair (no wonder I went bald so young!) and skeletal frame that stood in direct contrast to Dave. My physicality, or lack of it, coupled with my lapdog-like eagerness to please made Dave all the more attractive. Davey — silent, wild and free, like Davy Crockett, except he didn't wear a coonskin cap, he wore a helmet when the law made it mandatory. And under it, he folded a big red hanky into a triangle and tied it around his scalp. He said it kept him from getting "ha-ha-hat" hair, and yes, Davey's auburn curls flowed like lava across his back. When he hung his head forward to light a smoke, his hair swung to either side of his face like a copper curtain. And he would look up at those girls with his diamond blue eyes and smile like the devil. That's what they would have seen.

Of course, I saw it too and was not a little envious.

But that was before the fire.

It was a 1948 green International Harvester — a half-ton pickup truck — back when half-tons could actually haul a thousand pounds over the rear axle. Dave intended to fix it up and perhaps put a camper on the back so he could hunt and fish without worrying about having to set up or dismantle a wet tent. However, before he started with a hammer and saw, he thought it might be a good idea to see if the truck would run. In our living memory, it had sat in the backyard of a neighbour who suddenly needed to move things fast. He'd been charged under the municipality's Unsightly Premises Act.

Dave paid the guy ten dollars to haul it to our backyard right next to Mom's carefully cultivated vegetable plot in which she grew, among other things, ten-inch carrots straight as a die. The neighbour also kept pigeons and they had used the truck as a roost — inside and out. Dave and I shovelled out the front seat and lay newspaper on it. We also had to scrape fossilized pigeon shit off the steering wheel and dashboard. It took a day alone to clean the gauges, of which there were four, if you included the speedometer — fuel, battery and oil pressure. The speedometer went up to eighty — that would have been *miles* per hour, kilometres hadn't crossed the ocean yet. If the truck ever reached that speed, it would have disintegrated.

Dave was satisfied that the engine wasn't seized after soaking the piston heads with WD–40 poured liberally through the sparkplug holes. We cranked the engine physically with an actual hand-crank — a common device pre-1950. He muttered all the while about compression ratios and valve clearances, stuff I knew nothing about. He never stuttered when he talked mechanics. It was like singing to him.

Dave then clamped the leads to the six-volt battery and told me to kick the starter switch. (The keys were long gone, but Dave hot-wired the ignition.) But try as we might, the old truck would not start. So Dave spun the wing nut that held the air filter cover in place, removed it, and splashed fresh gasoline straight into the carburetor. I sat in the driver's seat, trying to ignore the residual pigeon shit, ready to step on the starter switch as soon as Dave gave the signal.

"Go!" he yelled.

The instant my foot made contact with the switch to pass the current from the battery through the coil and onto the spark plugs . . .

BOOM!

Dave was ablaze.

The flash knocked him back against the garage wall while flames ate at his shirt and hair, his beautiful hair. He beat his arms against his chest, flapping like a wounded bird in feathers of flames, spinning and bouncing off the garage wall. He could not see what was happening to his hair.

I jumped from the truck and tackled him, ripping the shirt off his back and rolling with him in the backyard dirt across the path and into the vegetables where the black loam was still moist with freshly sprouting rows of peas, lettuce, and carrots. The absurd thought that Mom would not be pleased crossed my mind so that I actually tried to roll back onto the path, beating Dave at the same time.

All this happened in silence, as though sound did not exist. But when the flames were out and Dave and I were sitting on the ground, Dave whimpered in shrill, short bursts — and the truck hummed, idling idiotically nearby.

Dave's eyebrows and lashes were gone. His nose, forehead and scalp were blistered red; skin hung from his wrists. Black knots of charcoal dangled like beads from his head.

"Fuck, it hurts," Dave whispered, as though making sound hurt him more.

"Let's get you to the hospital," I said.

"I might die," Dave said.

"No, you won't," I said.

"I want to," Dave said, his lashless eyes all the more blue in their nakedness.

"Davey, don't," I said. I could see Davey eight years old, rocking in the bedroom.

Dave then held his burnt hands in front of his face, turning their raw redness front to back. "No fingerprints," he whispered, a garish smile hanging on his beautiful lips. There were tears in his eyes, though.

I was yet again unscathed.

But in that moment, the unfairness of it all hit me, and I knew I would forever be in debt to Dave and that I would never be able to pay him back, that I was responsible for as much of Davey's sad, impossible life as anyone. In that moment, I wished we were at the lake where Dave was safe and wild.

⟶ ⟶

In the hospital, none of those girls ever came to visit. Dave didn't miss them. His biker friends did, though. They scared me shitless because I couldn't tell when they were joking and when they were not. They tolerated me because I was Davey's brother. After he was out, they bought him special, fine-grained gloves made out of kangaroo skin with really fine stitching to make sure the wrenching did not hurt his hands — well, too much. His hair grew back — most of it, anyway — a tight tangle of rusty wire. "Wolf hair," he called it.

It wasn't at all like wolf hair, but I got the point.

And all this happened long before he gave me the greasy note for "Didi," Dianne, our sister.

2

One of Harold's tricks is letting the pressure build on his bladder. The pain becomes exquisite after a time and helps him stay awake. It's an old habit from when he used to make long hauls — oranges and grapefruit from Florida, garlic, onions, and lettuce from Texas, tomatoes, avocados, and bananas all the way from Tepic, Mexico. He owned a refrigerator reefer then. The money was good and the fuel was cheap. He could go four or five hours without a stop, pissing in a bottle along the way. Time was of the essence. He still owns the Kenworth W900L, but she's old now, leaks a bit — like him. She's good enough for these short runs though, with her tandem axles and 475 horses for thirty-six feet of crushed stone — forty tons or so. He's not quite sure. There are no weigh scales here, but you do have to go a bit slower, shifting through almost all ten gears up and down the hills, the road cutting through black spruce and Precambrian shield south of Mahihkan Lake.

It's hardly been an hour and Harold knows he isn't going to make it to where he can relax in front of a urinal. The pressure is more than he needs to keep him awake. It's those damn little pink pills, not the Benzedrine he'd done in the old days, but the hydrochlorothiazide that the doc prescribed. "Piss pills," he calls them, making him do just that every twenty minutes before his eyeballs pop out — or so it seems.

They also keep his arteries from seizing up.

Harold imagines the whole system attached to his heart is like a radiator hose you leave too long. It grows crusty on the inside and brittle with age, till one day it gets too hot and blows sweet-smelling green coolant all over the road. And if you aren't paying attention, the whole block will glow red and you'll throw a rod through the head. They will tow you away. Double cherries flashing on top of the tow truck.

He approaches a long grade with a slight curve to it — he can't quite see the crest yet, partly because of the curve and partly because of the grade. Harold begins to gear down the five or six speeds he knows he needs to get it there, and once over, it'll be another half-hour before the turnout where he can stop to check his air brakes and tires.

Wishing he could wait till then, he glances at the bottle holder dancing on the dashboard. It holds an empty bottle of Lipton's tea. He's switched from Coke a year or two back because he likes the larger opening — it's easier to pee into.

As he's completing his downshifts, he checks his rear-view mirror and is surprised to see a single light approaching. *One-eyed monster, or bike?* he wonders. *Who'd be riding a bike this early in the day, this far north?* There's never much traffic on this road. The 8:30 bus should be coming down from La Ronge any minute, but other than that eventuality, he's only seen a couple of nondescript pickups going south. Judging by the shuddering headlight in his rear-view, he decides it is indeed a bike — a hard tail maybe, something with a very stiff suspension.

He takes the empty bottle, unscrews the cap, and makes an "O" with it in his mouth. He stuffs the bottle under his arm then unzips his fly. Retrieving the bottle, he cradles it together with the end of his penis to ensure an efficient coupling.

Harold glances again in the mirror but has lost the bike to the curve in the hill.

He feels the warm release of his bright yellow urine into the bottle. But the relief is brief.

The bus breaks over top of the hill.

Harold realizes his timing is lousy. He's going to need to get his hand on the gearshift before it's done with the bottle. He's going to have to squeeze it off mid-stream. Stopping is harder than starting.

As the bus approaches, a light flashes in his rear-view mirror. Is it the bike? Can't be. It was too far back. The bus driver is looking intently ahead. He often waves. Not today.

Harold manages to place the bottle back into its holder without spilling too much on his hand. He notices the urine looks almost the same as the tea. He quickly removes the cap from his mouth and jams it back onto the bottle, then spits and roughly wipes his lips on the back of his sleeve. *I could have had a lapful of piss. Might as well have pissed my pants and save myself the grief!*

The bus passes. He feels the slight buffet of backdraft from the two large vehicles passing in opposite directions. Harold is relaxed now — in control. One hand on the wheel, the other ready on the shift. He is going over the hill now, gaining speed. There is nothing in the mirror. He smiles to himself. *Bikers got bladders too.*

3

Day thirty-one, the sun rises like a Black Mouth Cur looking for his food dish. Sniffs around, pokes his nose into the kibble, and nibbles a crunch or two. Sighs, lies down — one eye half open. Sees me and Dianne in her car.

Dianne's driving. It's a new Saab. Silver. The colour of good dental work.

My own teeth are rotten. The reason I drink, I sometimes say but have to admit I don't need a reason. I do it because I'm an addict. I know that step one is admitting you're out of control, and that there are eleven more, but they're irrelevant.

Oh whisky bottle, please be my friend. I'd sing it now, but Dianne would object. It would be in bad taste considering the circumstances — being driven home from rehab. Besides, it would draw attention. Dianne objects to things that draw attention even though she tries not to. She's aware of the paradox. However, she bites her tongue. She smiles demurely — falsely. She is dressed in green, the colour of camouflage. The colour of her eyes.

It's not quite fall — cool and airy. Dianne travels across town in her husband's Saab to fetch me. I could have taken a bus, perhaps should have taken the bus. I am a bus person now. Dianne knows this. This means she has an agenda. It's in a green garbage bag in the trunk of the Saab. I have accepted the ride because I too have an agenda.

We don't say much because there's not much *to* say. Or rather there's too much to say and we don't know where to start. How to start. Instead, we watch the old yeller dog in the sky watch us. It's late August, just before noon. Everything is burnt and brown. The trees are strained by all the effort of summer. Their leaves grow weary of hanging. Soon enough, they'll let go.

I have a song running through my mind and I can't quite remember what it is or where it comes from. It loops in fragments. Was it something I wrote, or just something I covered? All I get is a scrap of melody and a shade of a lyric, "water", something, something "flowing slow". "Slow" or "free"? I don't know what it is. It'll bother me all day. This happens more and more lately. I wonder if it means anything. The prelude to Alzheimer's? Does it run in the family? Or is this just what happens when you begin to recognize that you're growing old?

Or is this what happens when your brother dies?

I repeat the phrase out loud and ask Dianne if it reminds her of anything.

"No," she says. She appears to be deep in thought. She purses her lips in and out, guppy-like. Our mother had a similar mannerism. It makes me smile.

I lean against the window and half close my eyes. I study her for a while. She does not have Mom's face. She doesn't seem to have Dad's either. The milkman's? Mom had been a very beautiful woman — in her day — exceptional, really. But not now. Alzheimer's is not pretty.

I have never thought of my sister as overly attractive, at least never consciously. A stranger might see her differently — would not, as the saying goes, kick her out of bed for eating crackers, especially considering her age, forty-five. She looks tough and rather boyish, although not without a style. I am certain of this because of an event that once happened.

Standing on the corner of Third Avenue and 22nd Street, waiting for the light to change, I noticed a woman, also waiting, across the street. She stared straight ahead, focusing on the walk light, her head slightly cocked, as though weighing one side of her thoughts. She stood taut and square to the ground, but displayed a quirky flare — style — in an odd green plaid that would have been garish on most. As the light changed and we walked towards each other, Dianne with her eyes cast downward still in thought, it wasn't till she had passed me that I realized it was my own sister. I felt stupid for an instant and then embarrassed because I found her attractive. Desirable.

By the same token, she did not even recognize me.

Yet it was a nice way to see your sister, unobserved and through the eyes of a stranger.

When I think about it now, it's how you'd expect her to look, having been pummelled by two older brothers, taunted and teased till she'd kick one of us, or tell Dad — which always took the fun out of it. You never knew what *he* was going to do, but there was a good chance it would involve violence — and alcohol, of course. He was only sober during actual working hours — a good, functioning alcoholic. I don't take after him at all. I am a bad, not-so-functioning alcoholic. However, if genetics are truly a factor, I inherited that particular propensity from him. But not the violence. That was all his. He beat both Dave and me, but not with the regularity Mom focused on Dave.

Neither parent ever touched Dianne. She was the youngest by five years — barely fifteen when I left home. While she was pummelled and beaten regularly but never maliciously by us in horseplay, we equally doted on her. She was our baby sister, nevertheless bruised for life to carry the tough and boyish attitude she built to emulate us and protect herself. That was our mark on her. The stylish aspect, however, is all her own, a way to distinguish herself — what, in fact, she does for a living — design things. The flaming red in the middle of the Sun Pine logo — the one with the tree — Dianne's; the arrow that points the way in the Super Express logo? — hers too — examples of winsome, money-in-the-bank, infamous clichés of commerce. They have made her wealthy. She can afford good dental work.

As we approach my place, the streets narrow into a semi-industrial neighbourhood, with scowling flat-roofed storefronts and cracked stucco faces. Low rent zones, the last to have their potholes fixed after the brittle winter freeze-ups. The heavily patched roads rattle the Saab. We pass a large shirtless man sitting on the stoop of a grimy clapboard house. He is playing with a small white dog. The dog is shaking a toy rat.

"That *was* a toy rat that dog was shaking, wasn't it?" Dianne asks hopefully.

"You never know in this neighbourhood. I'm on the next left."

"I know the way," says Dianne brusquely.

Dianne has taken my direction as somehow condescending. I guess there'd be no end to it — feeling patronized — no matter how long you lived. You'd always be second, or in Dianne's case, third — the youngest.

I suppose it's a tiny treasure the time I saw her on the street and didn't recognize who she was, and at the same time enjoyed the moment in ironic anonymity. I can't help but chuckle.

"What are you laughing at?"

"Oh, nothing. Just thinking."

I'm thinking of another time at the release party for *Hiding* where, standing around full of myself and even fuller of whatever it was they were passing around, I attempted to introduce Dianne to my partner, Rick; however, I could not remember her name.

"This is . . . ah . . . " I went blank. Her name had departed from that part of my brain where names are stored, and as the blood rushed passed my ears, Dianne kicked me, hard, on the shin. " . . . Dianne! My sister, Dianne!" The sudden violence loosed my memory.

"You asshole," she said and stomped out.

Although she never reminds me of the incident, verbally, I sometimes fear she's thinking of it — defensively — as in, "You can't even remember my name and I'm the only sister you have."

I decide to bring it up.

"Remember that time I couldn't remember your name?"

"What time was that?" She makes it sound like it happened more than once.

"At that album launch, remember?"

"What album launch?"

"*Hiding* — how many albums have I launched?"

35

"I never went to your album launch," she says.

"Yes, you were there, and I couldn't remember your name."

"That was at a concert where you introduced me to Rick."

"Oh."

Interesting how our memories can be so different.

"I've driven by your place to pick up Kirsten," she says. This is to explain how she knows where I live. I try to imagine where Kirsten would spend her time in this neighbourhood. "The mall," adds Dianne, reading my thoughts, or more likely, the perplexity on my face.

I nod. Yes. the mall. I'd forgotten about the mall. It's new — well, five-years old. I've never been there. My relationship to the world of consumerism is sparse. And I'm annoyed that they've removed half of this old neighbourhood putting through a freeway exchange. Progress. In with the new, out with the old. Making room for cars. Parking. ParKING.

Although I have not specifically invited her up to my apartment, I do not object when she pulls up in front of the paint store and turns off the ignition to the Saab. I know that Dianne wants to reveal her agenda, and I equally want to reveal mine — the delicate matter involving Dave's rather cryptic, short missive. I had read it almost immediately following Dave's last visit, justifying that anyone who gives you a letter and then drives under a gravel truck really intends you to read it too, even if it's addressed to someone else. Still, I don't understand the contents. Who is Jimmy Matheson?

We climb the stairs to my apartment. I am not the sole inhabitant above the paint shop and my apartment squats at the dark end of a meandering hallway through various sour smelling zones of corn mixed with urine. No air. An ascent into hell. Dianne holds her breath, a difficult task while lugging a large green garbage bag.

I tote a guitar case and backpack. The backpack contains twenty-eight days' worth of laundry — which is one pair of pants, two t-shirts and two pairs of black underwear. Yes, and some books. The guitar case contains Mr. Martin, a 1968 Martin D–18.

Every musician's instrument has a story attached. Some involve a burning building, like B.B. King's Lucille, some have travelled across centuries in and out of the hands of great musicians, some are not quite so exotic but have survived the music wars bearing scars. My guitar was a gift from Dave. Mr. Martin is worth three or four thousand dollars by now but it didn't cost David a cent because he stole it. He says he found it, but you don't "find" Martin D–18s.

"It fe-fe-fell off a t-t-ruck," he says.

"They don't fall off a truck and look like this." I note its pristine condition — no wear on the fret board, no scratches on the body and most notably — to me at least — no fingerprints. I hate a smudgy guitar.

"Fe-fe-fell into my hands," says Dave, holding his palms out, skyward — surrendering his purportedly fingerprintless fingers.

"Dave, you *have* fingerprints." I know he is trying to show me his thievery cannot be traced.

"F'ckoff!" he says, in a single syllable.

"No, really. They always grow back." I read this somewhere.

He looks at his hands. "Holy shit," he says.

And I know he is thinking about changing careers from thieving and wrenching to something that won't leave the same tracks. You can see it on his face, like, "What am I going to do now?" He doesn't say it, of course.

◦—◦

Dave was a great supporter of my music career, back when I had one. He even supported the semblance of one that came later, after my brief stint in the limelight. He'd show up at the most obscure places, which were most places I played — not being on the A circuit, or even the B. It was really more the X circuit — the bars, saloons, and lounges with cigarette burns on the tables, bar, and urinals, all ruined even further now by karaoke machines — if they're around at all.

I worked in those days when bar owners hired me because I worked for scale or less, and was a solo act who'd had a hit LP. Somebody would always walk in, recognize me and stick around till I sang it to them — "Hiding", Icegate's title track, one-hit wonder — usually late in the evening, the second-last song of my last set. This too made the bar managers happy — the longer the bar patrons sat waiting for their song, the more they drank. Del Shannon would be playing down the street singing his falsetto "Runaway" and "Hats Off to Larry" to forty people, and I would be bawling out "Hiding" to ten — if I was lucky. I'd gig in Dartmouth, not Halifax; Sutherland, not Saskatoon; St. Albert, not Edmonton. I made it as far west as the Shark's Tooth in New Westminster, but never all the way onto Granville Island.

Invariably, though, Dave and a bunch of his biker buddies would show up and terrorize the joint, wherever it was. The place would empty within half an hour as Dave and his buds horked on the floor, pissed in the sinks, and generally raised a din — which they didn't always do. But even when they behaved themselves — hid their knives and guns — their presence terrified the regular patrons as well as the owners and managers alike. I'd pretend not to know them and gained something of a reputation for being especially brave in the face of apparent great danger. No one could figure out how I attracted such a tough crowd. I kind of enjoyed it. Dave and I would have a little wink at one another and that would be about it — except if there was broken glass on the floor. Then I wouldn't look at him at all.

I did make a half-hearted attempt at finding the guitar's original owner by posting a note in the AF of M newsletter, local 709. There were a couple of queries but no one came close to the serial numbers. If Dave forged them, he did a good job. I never made inquiries from the Martin Company itself to identify the purchaser by way of tracking it down. I sometimes think I still should, that the guitar is too good for me. But I won't.

It's one of the few things I own that I don't wear on my back.

"You could have thanked me for the ride," says Dianne.

"It's a miracle we made it. You should get your brakes fixed."

"My brakes are fine."

"Then why'd you keep running red lights?"

"They weren't red, they were yellow."

I refuse to get into the technical fine points that determine it is just as illegal to run *amber* lights as red ones, because the mere fact that she calls them *yellow* means that the not-so-fine print in the Highways Traffic Act is irrelevant to Dianne. She certainly knows the difference between yellow and amber. It's her business to know the difference. It's what she does for a living — select colours. She'd better know the difference.

Although I have to admit that she is right — I could have thanked her for the ride.

"You didn't have to pick me up," I finally counter.

"I know that. But I did, didn't I?"

"You didn't have to."

"I don't have to do anything."

Dianne has an answer for everything. Even if she doesn't have an answer, she has an answer; you would have to get up by dawn to outmanoeuvre her which puts me at a distinct disadvantage because the last time I saw the sun rise, it was because I hadn't gone to bed. Musicians are not morning people. Neither are drunks.

Dianne is beholden to no one, least of all me — notwithstanding her relationship with her family — Kirsten and "the Doink." Still, she *intervenes* — commits me to Waldon. She owes me nothing, not even the truth, I think. I'm not always that certain what "the truth" is.

The truth about the Saab, for instance. It perplexes me why she drives as if it has no brakes and one gear — high, fast — like Dave. If she lived like she drove, she'd be gone too. Maybe she's just more skilled at driving. She's definitely more skilled at living. Her impulses are impeccable.

We reach the door of my apartment and I attempt to push through. The door does not budge. It appears to be locked. I set things down and begin the search for keys. I continue the discussion. "Okay, if you don't have to do *anything*, then why did you?" I ask.

"Because we have to get this done." She indicates the green garbage bag, which she plops onto the floor. It makes an "ooph" sound as though there's somebody inside.

"There's nothing in that bag for me," I say.

"Denny, I went through a lot of trouble to get this bag, and you're going to sort it with me if it's the last and only thing we ever do together, whether you're interested or not, because I was the one who went to his apartment and cleaned it out."

"And that's all you got?" I nudged the bag with my toe. I was still fumbling for keys.

"There wasn't much there. A greasy little man who claimed to be the landlord's agent let me in. The place looked like it had been ransacked. There were no signs of David, like his tools or anything, except for a bong and stash of pot hidden in the kitchen cabinet that I flushed down the toilet."

"You flushed his bong?"

"It went to the dump with the rest of his garbage. Everything else went to the Salvation Army Thrift Store. This, however," she poked the bag with a painted toe, "I saved for you."

"Clothes?" In the first place, Dave and I had totally different body types, but equally to the point, I have absolutely no interest in wearing a dead man's clothes.

"Some shirts and his jacket."

"Listen we can leave them right there and some of the neighbours will be glad to have them."

41

"You'd rather see some stranger wearing Dave's clothes?" Dianne tries a different tack.

"They're not strangers, they're neighbours." Although I'd be hard pressed to name a single one.

"He was your brother!"

Technically this is not true and Dianne is well aware of the fact, but even if it were, the discussion is unsettling, on top of which I am still somewhat shaky within my new sobriety. I struggle to fit the key into the lock. "Damn this thing." This lock is keeping me from proceeding with the rest of my life, whatever its shape. The metaphors are amplifying — the sun dog, *water* something, something *flowing free*, and I can't get the damn door open.

"Let me try," says Dianne.

"No." It somehow does my soul good to continue solo with this absurd struggle with a key and a lock. Perhaps this is what I am meant to do. Maybe I'll die there. That would be okay. I have to do it somewhere.

"Why is it locked?" asks Dianne.

This is a perfectly good question, now that I think of it, since I was not the one to lock it. I suspect, however, that it is not the real question; the real question is, *Why isn't Twyla here?* Twyla, Dianne's intervention co-conspirator in admitting me for rehab at Waldon. I answer the real question.

"I don't know, Dianne, why Twyla's not here. She's never here."

This is only a slight exaggeration since most people aren't home at this time of day. They have things to do, places to be — jobs, careers, professions. Twyla, however, has none of these things. I have no idea where she is.

"What's her problem?" Dianne asks. There's a nasty edge to her voice. She's somehow taken Twyla's absence is a personal affront.

"Jesus, Dianne, what's *your* problem?" Dianne's question rankles as though Twyla's not being home could possibly be a problem. The last time I saw her was twenty-eight days ago. She never came to visit me. I understand that. Waldon is not a place in which she would feel the least bit comfortable.

However, the discussion refocuses my attention to the task at hand and the heavy click of the lock lets me burst through the door. The air is cool and stale, an improvement over the hallway, but I don't remember it smelling like this — fresh cigarette smoke is far more bitter. But there is another scent, something missing or something present, I can't put my finger on it. Twyla? What does Twyla smell like? Sour. She has a sour smell. Alcohol, sour and sweaty. And tobacco, of course. What do I smell like? You can't smell yourself — unless you're starting to rot. Which does happen.

I want a cigarette, and a drink, even though it's barely past noon my first day out. I should have other things on my mind, laundry, the power bill. Phone. The phone was disconnected before. Wasn't it? No. That was how I heard about Dave. I shouldn't be thinking about booze and cigarettes. It's all I think about.

I sit at the table and take out my tobacco and papers.

Dianne sits in my Sally-Ann-rescued easy chair, and opens the bag.

I'm shaky. It seems to come and go. I can live with it. It's the way things are for me, but I hate Dianne to see me like this. It was okay in the car. Why is it showing now? Or is it showing? What can she see?

"I worry about you," she says.

"Well don't." She sees something, that's what. Maybe everything.

"Really, I thought I'd check with you before I took this to the Sally Ann."

"Sally would be very happy to have it," I say.

"What about this?" She pulls Dave's black leather jacket from the bag. "It's almost new."

"Keep it. Give it to the Doink."

"I wish you wouldn't call him that."

"I wish he wasn't one."

"Steve's allergic to black."

"He allergic to a *colour*?"

"As a matter of fact, yes, and very."

I understand how Dianne's husband, Steve, the Doink, might object to black — too sinister. But to actually be allergic to it is pushing things. I suppose that explains the silver Saab — its colour at least, but not why you'd choose something so unsuited to the Canadian winter, a car from a company the keeps going bankrupt. I cannot imagine how Steve and my sister met, much less were attracted to each other enough to create offspring. True, it might have only happened once, producing their daughter, Kirsten. It's amazing enough for any two people to get together; we sniff each other out like most gendered life forms, pollinate, and die — all the result of pheromones. It has nothing to do with love and everything to do with natural selection. But, even Darwin would have winced if he saw Dianne and the Doink together.

Kirsten, however, is really the predictable product of such a union. She managed to inherit what each parent considers the worst in the other, which makes the poor girl intolerable to them but which most people don't mind at all or actually find attractive. To which my sister replies, "I don't want to dress my daughter in leather; it's morbid."

"Leather isn't morbid, Dianne. In fact, some people think it's rather exciting."

"You know what I mean. I can just see her — traipsing around in her dead uncle's jacket. She would think it was so cool." She tosses the jacket at me.

I can't see anything wrong with this. If somebody had asked me to wear my dead uncle's black leather jacket when I was thirteen, I'd have been thrilled, Navy issue or not, assuming that my late Uncle Frank's leather jacket was Navy issue. I once saw a picture of him sitting on a motorcycle in front of a large ship wearing a military police helmet. My cousin, though, said he was never in the navy. So I don't know what the story is — how the incriminating picture of my uncle came to be, or whether I just fantasized the whole thing. I don't think so, though. So much to know, so little time to know it.

I'm examining it now, stretching it out in my arms. "He wasn't wearing this," I say, turning it over.

"What do you mean?"

"Well I'm no in forensic expert, but a jacket that's been tangled in the wheels of truck at 120 kilometres an hour is not going to look like this. It's not going to look like much of anything. And there's likely to be bits of body attached to whatever is left."

Dianne's eyes grow wide in recognition. "You're right. When you're right, you're right. He must have had two. Or maybe it came off at impact."

"What do you mean?"

"Haven't you ever noticed all those shoes lying around after an accident?"

"No."

"The broken glass? The coolant, you know, fluids — sometimes blood. And shoes."

"No, actually, I haven't. I don't stand around gawking at car wrecks."

"You don't know what you're missing."

"I know exactly what I'm missing, Dianne. And that's why I don't stand around gawking." She is taking a perverse pleasure in this.

"Well anyway, people's shoes come off. I guess we very suddenly change shape at impact."

"And you're calling me morbid."

"That's not morbid. That's just being observant. We're like water balloons — we change shape when we're thrown around. And actually . . . " She is building towards something here. Something to do with changing shape. I hand the jacket back to her.

"Actually, what?"

"Nothing," says Dianne.

The discussion is not really about Dave and his jacket. It's about me. Dianne is thinking that I am closer to death than she'd care to speculate — at least in front of me — no doubt because of certain habits I enjoy. She folds the jacket on her legs but does not put it back into the bag.

There is something amiss in my apartment but I can't put my finger on it. I am numbed by the staleness and lack of texture. It needs the fresh scent of burning tobacco to sting the eyes and provide a little substance.

"You don't mind if I smoke, do you?" It's a rhetorical question, designed more to annoy than to seek permission.

"I don't care if you burst into flames." One of our mother's old jokes, and not too funny when Dave was around. Dianne, though was too young to realize why her biggest brother and had moved from the garage to the hospital and what had happened to his hands, hair and face.

I light my hand-rolled cigarette and life is tolerable again, at least for the first drag. There is a snide reason why I ask Dianne if I can smoke in my own abode. The last time I lit up in front of her, she almost had me arrested for precipitating the Doink's asthma attack on a restaurant's outdoor patio where I assumed it was safe, and legal. Sad. Where the hell are you supposed to have a smoke these days? You can hardly turn around without someone complaining and whining and threatening the law. People should develop a little more tolerance. Maybe bursting into flames isn't so stupid after all. But then, nothing is as it seems. Maybe Dianne is really is lamenting Dad who died of lung cancer after forty-eight years of smoking two packs a day. That he had refused treatment too. "I brought it on myself," he'd said. You had to admire that. There wasn't much more about him to admire.

I wonder if these ritual suicides run in the family.

Dianne has risen to sit in the other of my two kitchen chairs, not so subtly picking apart my apartment. She seems to be pondering what else to say, and I'm blowing smoke rings. I'm not trying to make her uncomfortable, but I'm not going out of my way to put her at ease either — I'm not sure why; I have questions too.

"You know, you've never invited me up here before," she says.

"I didn't invite you up here now." Technically, this is a joke; literally, it's the truth.

"It's . . . " she looks for a descriptor, "very *tidy*, Dennis."

"Sparse," I correct. "The boxes make it look tidy."

"What's in them?"

"Junk. Old gear. Where I keep my messes."

"And this . . . " She reaches down to heave aside my backpack but stalls; it's heavier than she expects.

"God! What's in here?"

"Underwear. And books. They had a library there. I took a bunch."

"To read?"

"No, to sell on the street corner. Yes, of course to read. They're supposed to inspire me to turn my life around — full of twelve-step nonsense."

"Good for you, Denny."

"It's shit. It's for people who believe in God or some higher form of being — 'a power greater than ourselves' is the actual phrase. 'Turn our will and our lives over to the care of God *as we understand Him*'. I might not have much, but my *will* is still my own. I am not about to give it up."

"And that, of course, lets you off the hook."

"I just don't believe in higher life forms. What's wrong with lower life forms? Why not them? Who rates life forms anyway? It gets so complicated, Dianne. I just can't cope."

"So why did you drag them up here, then?" She actually opens the bag and pulls one of the books out.

"I don't know. Trying to cover for the ones I stole? Too polite to say no to the ones they gave me? It was one of Mom's rules, 'Always accept what you're offered'."

"'Never look a gift horse in the mouth' is what she actually said. *"Reflexiones Diarias',"* she reads. *"'Esto es un libro de reflexiones escritas por los AA para los AA . . . .'* This is in Spanish!"

"I thought I should get something out of the damn thing — maybe pick up a phrase or two."

She opens the book. "'Cesar Guzman.' You stole Cesar's book?"

"It was sitting on a shelf with a pile of others. We were encouraged to help ourselves. It was a gift." From Cesar, I guess.

"Yes, well, that's exactly what this jacket is, Denny, a gift. Would you at least try the damn thing on?" Segueing this into a kind of opportunity, she drops the book on the bag, stands, and unfolds the jacket again.

"It is not a gift. It is pillage. Why do you want me to wear this jacket so bad?"

"Mostly because you don't seem to want to."

"Okay, *bueno.*"

I get to my feet and put on the heavy leather jacket that smells faintly of dog. Dave used to hate dogs, especially little ones — Chihuahuas — yappy things he'd sooner dropkick than pet. Dogs seemed to know how he felt about them. They'd give their warning bark or shy away. They rarely ignored him. Yeller did, though. Exception to prove the rule.

"Smells," I say.

"I know. It's funny," she says, "that it should smell so doggy when he wouldn't have anything to do with them.

Kirsten's almost as bad, but at least she's not allergic to leather."

"You say that like someone in your house is."

"Quite severely, actually."

We both know she is talking about The Doink.

"So you have no leather in your house."

"None."

"No shoes — anything?"

"Nothing."

"How does the guy run marathons when he can barely breathe?"

"The jacket looks good on you. It makes you look like him." She ignores my jibe.

"Thanks. I look like a dead man." I check the pockets. I once found five dollars in a Sally Ann jacket. You never know.

"I did that already," says Dianne. "They were empty."

"Ah, but did you know about the secret pocket behind the vest?" The pleat on the front vest conceals a small pocket zipper — standard location for the spare bike-key, which the pocket holds. It also contains a folded piece of paper. "Oh, what's this?" I unfold it.

Dianne leans over, curious to know what it says. "Hmm . . . tomatoes, cilantro, lime, and onion . . . Evidently he was making salsa."

"*Planning* salsa. He wouldn't need a list if he was actually making it." I wonder why he would write that down — like you could not remember tomatoes, cilantro, and lime, then of course, it occurs to me — he would hand the list to someone, a clerk, perhaps, because it would take him forever to say it. But then why would he not just grab it himself? It's not like the veggie counter at Loblaws is behind bars. I'm astonished enough that he wrote anything down because he was not into leaving tracks — unless they belonged to a Harley Davidson. Hence, two wheels, not four; hence fast, not slow; hence dead, not alive.

But he did leave more than a salsa recipe.

"Did you read the letter?" I ask.

"What letter?"

"The one I gave you twenty-nine days ago."

"You told me not to open it."

"Dianne, if I didn't want you to open it, I wouldn't have given it to you." *Trust Dianne to take me literally.*

When I said not to open it, I meant that it contained important information — a message, in fact, from Dave. I could never have guessed that she would do as she was asked. When she was a child, she always did the opposite of what Dave and I told her to do. "Don't follow us!" She'd be twenty steps behind. "Don't jump!" She'd be on her way to the ground. "Don't eat the black peanuts!" They'd be in her mouth. And no matter what trouble she would get into as a result, they would get the blame. "You're supposed to look after your sister." Dad, coming at us, loosening his belt.

"You said not to open it unless something happened to you, unless you didn't make it out. You weren't in very good shape, Denny."

I was not in very good shape. I made it to the funeral home — a bit early. I couldn't figure out why they wouldn't let me into the service. Nor could I understand why the place was locked up tighter than a drum. Apparently, there are rules against pounding on funeral home doors at 3:00 AM I couldn't figure out what the police were

51

doing there trying to talk to me when I was in no mood to listen. I think maybe I tried to chase them away. I quieted right down after they Tasered and took me to a cell where I finished the night. I could not stop shaking the next morning. I couldn't drink a coffee. I tried but it was useless. It was then that I let Dianne and Twyla park me at Waldon Centre for twenty-eight days, and it was then that I gave Dianne the letter, on the way to Waldon, on the way in.

"The police said you were crying and hollering his name."

"That was no excuse to Taser me. You could have had two dead brothers."

Davy, Davy Crockett, king of the wild frontier. I can't remember when I stopped calling him Davey and started calling him Dave. When Mom was really annoyed, she'd call him by two of his three names, David Allen — never his last — neither Givens nor Mackenzie. It was as though he didn't have one. He used either or both himself, depending on the situation.

I missed the entire funeral, well, memorial. A few of Dave's biker buddies showed up. His parole officer. The only family was Dianne and Kirsten and an ancient uncle who'd been a school teacher. That was it. Apparently the Doink sat in the Saab and waited for them.

"Yeah, I know. But weren't you curious?"

"Yes, I was curious. But I didn't want to know."

"You can't be curious and not want to know at the same time, Dianne. It doesn't make sense." Dianne is reminding me of our mom who would say things like, "I didn't make a mistake; I did it wrong," somehow distinguishing between the two.

"Lots of things don't make sense, Denny. That doesn't make them any less real."

"So, you've never opened it."

"No."

I fold and unfold the guacamole list — *avocado, cilantro, lime, tomato* . . . Should I just straight out ask her who Jimmy Matheson is? I can't bring myself to do it. I suspect she knows the contents of the Davey's note and doesn't want to talk about it. Yet.

"No garlic," says Denny.

"What?"

"It's missing from the list."

"Dave hated garlic," reminds Dianne. "He was allergic."

"Was he?"

"You don't remember his breaking out in blisters?"

"No — when?"

"You were still in high school — around your grad."

"That wasn't from garlic, Dianne — that was from his burn."

"What burn?"

"You're kidding." Did they keep this from her? How could they have? Why? "You don't remember his hair, his hands and his nose?"

"No — just his lips. I assumed the blisters were from garlic, but I didn't know it at the time. It's what happens to Steve when he goes near it. I thought they had something in common. You're saying he was burned?"

"His truck exploded on him. He was on fire. I put him out. I can't believe you don't remember the time he spent in hospital."

"I'd remember that, Denny. You're making it up."

53

I know I'm not making it up. Why would I make something like that up? The scent of gasoline and burnt hair conjures at the back of my throat as it does from time to time. A sudden flash of light will bring it there when I least expects it. Unbeckoned. Unwelcomed. Vintage International Harvester pickup trucks have the same effect. I am suddenly doubtful.

"You just don't remember," I say.

"I remember everything, Denny. I remember the last time you wrote me a letter."

"I wrote you a letter?"

"It was very short. It said, 'Dear Di, Feed the animals.'"

"That's not much of a letter."

"You didn't put yourself out, no."

"A dog and a cat — Yeller and . . . " It is coming back. *A dog and a cat, Yeller and . . .*

" . . . Leticia," Dianne reminds me.

"Yes, Leticia." The cat suddenly forms on the back of my eyeballs. "She was kind of a pinto, right?"

"Calico."

"The vainest cat in the world. Poor Yeller was second fiddle." I think of Yeller for a moment and his sad, piggy-doggy eyes. "Poor fucking Yeller."

"Why do you say that?"

"Dad shot him."

"What!"

"*Had* him shot — same thing."

"Dad had Yeller shot? I don't believe it."

"The RCMP came and put a bullet through his head."

"Why?"

"He ate the Unruh's rabbit." The Unruhs lived next door. They kept rabbits. A rabbit. "So Dad says, 'If this is what Yeller will do to a rabbit, what might Yeller do to small children?'"

"Why don't I remember this? I remember the rabbits. I don't remember Yeller getting shot."

"You don't remember Dave's burn. Some things we remember and some things — *most* things — we don't. You remember my letter, I don't. Selective memory, I guess." *Leticia.* I hadn't thought of Leticia in years. Why Leticia? Yeller was a dog's name. But Leticia was a rock 'n roll girlfriend. "O Leticia, you're stealing my heart away." Or a ship. *The HMCS Leticia.* Home port? Saskatoon. "Please whiskey bottle, please be my friend . . . " It should be *gin* bottle, but what the hell kind of poetry is that?

"Water, water / Flowing free" A line of lyrics pencils itself in.

"What?"

"I think it's a song. I think I'm working on it. That's how they come."

"I don't know it."

"I don't either."

"Is there a melody?"

"'Do-do, do-do, do-do, do-do', that's all I remember."

"Sounds like the *Twilight Zone.*"

"Everything sounds like *Twilight Zone* these days, Dianne." I begin to remove the jacket. "If this could talk, it would probably bark. It really does stink."

"So Dad shot Yeller. He bit me once, you know, and he made such a mess of the backyard."

"I was supposed to keep it clean but I wasn't very good at it." I hand the jacket back to her. "I used to hate spring when the snow had mostly gone leaving lumps of semi-desiccated doggy-doo, and I'd and pick my way through with a rake and some garbage bags like a sapper through a minefield. Mom would yell at me to get my ass in gear."

"Which you never did."

"No, I never did, did I? I always let her down."

"Everybody let her down."

"Except you."

"Except me." She stuffs the jacket back into the bag. "I hate doing this, you know. I wish there was some way to . . . " She pauses looking for the right word. " . . . Honour him. You know, acknowledge his life somehow."

"Give it to Mom, then. See what she does with it. She's the one who should do some honouring."

"She's in no position to do much of anything."

"Yeah? So how is she?"

"She's fine, I guess — considering the circumstances."

"Meaning?"

"She's in a wheelchair."

"I should give her a call."

"Yes, you should do that — not that she'd know who you are."

"I will. Later, when I'm a little more together." My cigarette has burned to a pinched stub, scorching my fingers. Looks like a roach. I stuff it among the ashes that fill a clamshell ashtray.

"She would have been glad you went in."

"Yeah, I bet."

"No, really, she would have prayed for you."

Mom would pray for anything. *She'd pray for better weather, for the Habs to win, for a good crib hand, for world peace. Her prayer knew no bounds. Was boundless . . . homeward bound, I wish I were . . .* "I know she would have. I wonder if she prayed for Dave?"

"Maybe, yeah. Who was the patron Saint of Lost Causes? Was it Jude? She'd pray to him — to intercede on Dave's behalf."

"Yeah, that was how it worked, you're right. And it would have done so much good."

"You mean for you, or for Dave?"

"Either of us."

"Well you could be worse off."

"How?"

"You could be dead, Denny. Like your brother."

"Not unless somebody shot me, Dianne, like, with a Taser."

"You are every bit as suicidal as Dave."

"Are you kidding? I love life! People kill themselves because they think death's an improvement, otherwise they wouldn't do it."

"She would have prayed for you anyway — that's what peasants do."

I look at Dianne, study her for a second. She does not look at me. She is picking something off her lap. I had no idea this was her opinion of our mother. I will have to recalibrate my opinion of her, of Dianne, that is. My opinions of my mother are very firm. "For all her praying, she was not really a very nice person," I say.

"She is still alive. Let her be."

Let her be, let her be. Speaking words of wisdom . . .

"Makes me feel guilty, that's all — like I'm her cross to bear. I need coffee. Do you want some?" The coffee, if there's any left, will be in the cupboard next to the stove that doesn't work — except for a single burner,

57

the perimeter of which is encrusted with eons of burnt offerings, a black halo.

"Sure. Dad was her cross to bear."

"Dad?" I open the cupboard door. It's not totally empty. The mouse turds aren't too deep.

"He wasn't home half the time. And the other half, they fought."

"Shit."

"No, it's true."

"I'm talking about the coffee. There is none. You want tea?"

"Sure. We should have stopped for groceries."

"Yeah." I neglect to mention that I don't have any cash and that I was hoping that Twyla might have at least stocked up on coffee. Tea. I hate tea. "I never knew they fought."

"Well, they did." Dianne has taken off her shoes and folded her feet beneath her. Planning on staying awhile?

"This is news to me. I thought he was too busy dying," I say, louder than normal to cover the hisses and bangs of the ancient plumbing as it coughs water into the kettle. I let it spit and ooze from the tap for a while, hoping to clear it of all the crud. Didn't Twyla run any water while I was gone?

Water, water . . .

"A lot happened between the time you left home and when he was diagnosed with cancer."

"Well I was home for sixteen years. Nobody fought then — I mean, aside from you and me." I put the water on the burner, turn the dial. It has one temperature — high. "What did they fight about?"

"Money. You. Me. Dave. Anything, really."

"Why would anyone fight about Dave? I thought everyone agreed he was a shit."

"I didn't think he was a shit."

"Yeah, well you don't think anyone's a shit."

"Yes I do."

"Who?"

"Don't push me."

"Yeah, okay. Except for me." I'm not sure she's just being rhetorical here, or if she really believes it. In which case, I am wondering why she is still here, trying to make herself comfortable, no less. Another recalibration.

"There's a lot you don't know, Dennis, because you weren't around."

"There's a lot I don't know, Dianne, because no one would tell me. Like Dave being in jail. No one ever told me Dave was in jail."

"You did so; you got his bail and everything."

"I'm talking about the first time he was in jail, before I came back — not his drug busts, or whatever they were. They were hauling him in every six months. He never would tell me."

"He was running girls."

"He was what?"

"He was a pimp."

"Jesus Christ, I didn't know that. How did you know?"

"I read the newspaper, Denny."

"Holy shit."

"And you don't?"

"No, Never."

"Never?"

"Once. The reason I know about the first time Dave was in jail. He sent me a newspaper clipping with all the gory details. He was damn lucky that guy didn't die or he'd still be in jail."

"At least he'd be alive."

"Everybody else knew about this: Mom, Dad, you and probably half of Saskatoon. Did everybody know he was a pimp?"

"Everybody but you, I guess."

"Jesus Christ — my brother the pimp. I don't know anything and I wouldn't have known about the first whatever if he hadn't sent me the paper. I think he was proud of it. How come no one told me?"

"You were in Cape Breton, raising sheep."

"So? I shouldn't know my brother's in jail?" This still makes me angry even though it's water under the bridge, *flowing free*. My brother the pimp. What's the point of having family if they keep all these secrets from you? "And I wasn't raising sheep, I was looking after them. I was writing too."

"You co-wrote one song. Big deal."

"I co-wrote *two* albums, including the behemoth mega-hit that I sang, by the way . . . "

"And I heard it every day."

" . . . and I wrote at least seven-eighths of that."

"I still hear it on elevators."

"It was recorded in eighteen languages. People are still figuring out ways to make money off it. There's a yodelling version from Switzerland that is playing on YouTube as we speak. It's depressing. I just thank God for SOCAN. That's how come I get cheques from time to time."

Unfortunately, they are very few and far between. But for the most part, they have kept me in gin and tobacco. I begin to sort my dresser drawers wondering if I've hidden something drinkable in there. I have sometimes done that to surprise and treat myself.

"Where's that tea you promised?"

"The water has to boil, Dianne."

"Well you have to turn the stove on for it to do that," she says.

"I did."

Dianne reaches across to the kettle. "How come it's still cold then?" she asks.

"Oh for shit's sake." I am at the stove now and can see that it's turned on, but that there is indeed no heat beneath the kettle. "The stove is fucked. None of the burners work."

"None?"

"None."

"How long have you had that thing?"

"I don't know. It came with the apartment."

"Call your landlord. Have him replace it."

"It's not his. It was left here by the people who lived here before." And the less I see of the landlord, the better. I am thankful that I have stashed his rent — last month's. I like to keep a month behind to ensure I retain my damage deposit.

"You can't live like this, Denny."

"Of course I can. I've been living like this all my life."

"I mean without a stove."

"There's more than one way to boil water. Voila! The microwave." I have an ancient microwave. It is quite possibly a health hazard since the micro seems to continue waving when I open the door. I have to turn it off first. I pour the water from the kettle directly into a matching pair of chipped cups — the chips match, not the cups — and plant them in the machine. I turn it on. It sounds like a vacuum cleaner.

Dianne shouts above the roar. "Twenty years ago there was lots of stuff we didn't know about you either, you know." Dianne is back at Dave-in-jail. She continues. "We knew you were alive because you had a song on the radio."

"If I'd have been in jail you would have heard about it, believe me."

"You didn't tell us the first time you were in the hospital."

"I did so."

"Not at the time, you didn't."

This is true. I waited till I got out before I told anyone I had been in. And unlike Dave, there was no running till I puked when I did. I was just ushered to the door in a wheelchair, then greeted by a cold, raw day with a fierce wind. I could barely stand. I had a truck back then, Dave's old International with a box on the back. I lived in it for a while. I remember the damn wind almost tumbled the homemade camper off the truck box — with me inside. Spring in Cape Breton. I think I wrote a song about it. *When the wind comes howling, I think of you . . .* It was a lie. The wind never made me think of anybody but me.

"I didn't want to upset anyone."

"The same reason Mom and Dad didn't mention Dave to you."

"It's not the same thing. And the reason it's not the same thing is because he wasn't covered in little red blotches from head to foot. His liver didn't shut down with all that crap having nowhere to go. Freaked me right out. I damn near died."

"I'm not surprised."

"I didn't want anybody to see me. I didn't even want to see myself."

"I don't think anyone would have flown out to Cape Breton to watch you fester, Den."

"Mom would have — if she had the money."

"I'm glad she didn't. Alcohol poisoning — it amazes me how you could have done that, Denny."

"You have to be pretty dedicated. I didn't know how to pace myself then." I didn't either. I was in all-out, full-out, drink-till-you-drop mode.

"What did you do, get drunk with your sheep every night?"

Somehow, people carry the impression that I once owned a flock of sheep and lived on a farm. It's an impression I have never attempted to clarify because it's harmless and I liked the misconception. Why diminish a myth? The *Hiding* songwriter. It added to my mystique. The truth of course is that when I wasn't inhabiting the back of my truck, I did have a sort of house in the boonies — a recycled barn made only slightly less cozy with the absence of cows and chickens. It had running water if you pumped it and electricity if you kept the battery charged. I had a small garden of stunted, weed-ridden vegetables that I gamely tried to grow for a couple of years. The neighbour's sheep kept trying to eat it. I thus became a sort of volunteer shepherd. Some people thought the sheep were mine. I let them believe it despite never owning a one. I had a dog for a while though, Boomhauer, a big, dumb black lab. The neighbour with the sheep shot him.

"No, I did not get drunk every night with the sheep, Dianne. They don't drink much. They were too busy eating. Did you know they were vegetarians?"

"Yes, I knew that."

"Like Hitler. And Twyla. Nazi sheep. I wonder where she is?"

A loud bell rings, the microwave telling me that I should turn it off or the before the chipped cups explode. The teabags are a bit crusty. I drop them into the hot water.

"So, she's a vegetarian."

"You bet."

"I'd never met her before . . . before Waldon."

Now it hits me. Dianne is hanging around to meet Twyla. And here I thought it was to sort through Dave's stuff.

"You're not missing much. She's a singer."

"Oh, that's what she does."

"No, that's not what she does, that's what she is."

"Well, what does she do?"

"I don't know. I've never been able to keep track." Twyla does as little as possible — always. During the eight months she's been with me, she's worked in a tanning salon, a tattoo shop, and two different restaurants. But singing is her passion and she's not half bad. She sits in on all the Saturday afternoon jams at Fudd's and has never been booed off stage. She likes to drink too. Something else we have in common. There's nothing like love in a bottle.

"This is a record-long relationship, and you don't know what she does?"

"No, Christine was the record. Twyla's not even a year. We were going to form a duo."

"Why don't you?"

"I don't know. We never get around to it." Rehearsing is hard when you're always hung over. It's even harder when you try to do it with someone. "She always seems busy with these mysterious tasks, day and night. I wonder where she is. I always knew where Christine was."

"I saw her the other day — Christine. She looked good."

"She always looked good. And she knew it, too."

"I wonder why she didn't go to the funeral."

"Because I was going to be there."

Dianne doesn't say anything right away because the irony that I wasn't there either wouldn't change anything, wouldn't explain Christine's absence too. Suffice it to say, we weren't rolling in the hay somewhere. But Christine and Dave had known each other for years. I think maybe they even dated. Dave introduced me to her, like he knew we'd get along — even though she was older than me. That was how we met.

"I wonder how many facelifts a person can have before their eyeballs pop out?"

"Don't talk to me about Christine."

"Sorry. You're the one who mentioned her."

"She broke my heart."

"You don't have a heart, Dennis. You have an enlarged liver."

I slop my tea getting to my feet to show her the door. "You should be going now," I say.

"That was a joke, Dennis. I was kidding. You're supposed to laugh."

"It's not funny. Don't kid. I *have* an enlarged liver."

"I'm sorry," she says.

"Don't be sorry, either. Sorry never fixed anything."

"You want anything else from the bag?"

"No."

"Do you need anything? Cash?"

"I'm fine."

She is definitely stalling and I just want to be alone now. I want some time to shake the flies from inside my head. They are buzzing. They travel from the top of my head to the centre of my chest. I know what will make them stop.

"I'd like to wait till Twyla gets back. I mean, if that's okay. I'd like to talk to her." She actually says it.

"Why?"

"Because I don't know her. Because I want to see who's looking after you — no, no, I don't mean that, not looking after you, looking *out* for you," she clarifies, digging herself further into a dark little pit. "Do I have to have a reason? Because Dave's been dead for a month, because we have to do something with his ashes, because Dad's been dead for ten years, because Mom is dying, because we're the only two left in the family and we don't know each other. That's why. Are those enough reasons?"

For the first time in my life, Dianne has spoken to me in words that have a kind of desperation and make her oddly vulnerable. I now suspect that I'm supposed to do likewise. I don't like being vulnerable. It's why I drink. No, that's not true. I drink because I'm an addict. It makes me pause, however, and normally I like pauses because there is nothing in them. Perhaps a bit of tension. But this one of filled with something I know very little about — remorse. I don't know if it's mine or hers.

"Yes. Those are reasons enough. I'm sorry."

"No, you're not. You don't know what sorry is," she says, then suddenly looks about the apartment. "Where's your bathroom?"

I indicate a beaded curtain that hangs over a doorway. I have no idea what happened to the actual door. It was missing when I moved in. Why would you take a door, especially to a bathroom? It occurs to me that some people might be uncomfortable using a doorless bathroom and that one of these people might be my sister. I have long since grown used to peering between the beads to watch the evening news — back when I had a TV. It just sort of disappeared. I do have a stereo however.

"Are you okay? Di? Yeah, listen, hang around awhile. I'll put on some tunes."

I am an artist. I pride myself in my powers of observation despite their diminished state under the constant pressure of drink, but it is only now that I see that my sound system — if I can flatter myself by calling it that — is missing.

"Holy shit, where's my stereo?" It isn't anywhere. It's nowhere in the room. Twyla has done a major furniture shift. "Where's . . . ? My CDs are gone too! My . . . everything's gone!"

Dianne pushes aside the beads and re-enters the room. She is reading a note.

"'Have a great life.'"

"What?"

She hands me the note. "It was stuck in the mirror."

"'I got a better offer. Have a great life. Sorry to leave like this.' Fuck. Fuck me cold. I'm having a great life! Isn't this a great life? What the hell next? Shit." Then it occurs to me what the hell might be next. In three steps, I am back at the cupboard where I pull down an old yogurt container and snap off the lid. From it, I retrieve a ten-dollar bill. "I don't believe it. I just don't believe it. She took my rent."

"What?"

4

Harold can't understand why the cherries are pulling him over. Except they don't use cherries anymore. Their red and blue lights jab left and right from behind the chromed front grill of a black SUV. What happened to the old days when you knew it was a cop's car — okay, RCMP cruiser? Cops are cops, even if they're Mounties. What do they want? He certainly hasn't been speeding. His brakes are good. The load is covered. All his lights are working, or were when he started up. His licence is good, so is the rig's. He knows they know. He knows them too — well, knows them to see them. Maybe even met one or the other before in town, and they see each other on this road at least twice a week. He watches them approach in his rear-view mirror, one on each side of his rig. The younger one (they're all young now) doesn't even look like a cop. He looks like he should be pushing buttons on a computer. Nerdy — complete with thick, black-rimmed glasses. Reminds him of his grandson, always with his nose in a book. Is this what he'll become? A cop? An officer of the law? A Royal Canadian Mounted Policeman? He doesn't call them pigs or screws; he has too much respect for the uniform. He actually calls them "sir" and doesn't like it when they stop him. He supposes he could do worse than having a grandson as a cop. He could be a dope pusher or a, a what . . . a homo or something. That would be worse.

He watches the grandson-like cop approach on the right, the passenger side of the rig. The slightly older cop at least looks like one. A flat, expressionless face. The beginnings of jowls hanging on each side of his chin. Harold imagines that in twenty years the cop will have the same paunch he does. He wonders if he'll have to take the same piss pills, which reminds him to roll the offending urine-filled tea bottle out of sight. But the flat-faced cop has stopped at the rear of the rig. He seems to be looking at something. Maybe one of his lights *has* blown.

He disappears behind the rig.

Suddenly, the grandson-like cop stops and turns around like he's been called. He walks to the back of the rig as well and disappears behind it.

Harold wonders if he should get out and join them to see what it is they're looking at. But he knows they don't like that. They want you to stay in your vehicle, even harmless old farts like himself.

Finally, the jowly cop comes out from behind the truck and starts towards the cab. The nerdy one heads back to the cruiser. Harold is curious to hear what they have discovered at the back of his rig.

Rolling down his window, Harold leans out. "What can I do you for?" he asks.

"You didn't see a motorcycle twenty or thirty kilometres back did you, Harold?"

Harold is surprised the cop knows his name. He knows he met him someplace but can't remember where. Maybe it was the Co-op, but you don't meet people at the Co-op, you just see them there. Maybe the curling rink, then. Must have been the curling rink.

"I saw one on my tail, but he never passed — why?"

"Maybe you better come back here."

Harold climbs down from the cab and follows the jowly cop to the back of the trailer. And there, lodged behind one of the rear axles between the brake hoses, is a boot, a black leather boot.

"How the hell did that get there?" asks Harold.

The nerdy cop raises his eyebrows and looks at the jowly cop who shrugs his shoulders. "We're going to have to charge you with failure to stop at the scene of an accident, Harold."

"What accident?"

"The one that lodged that boot in your brake hose," says the young nerdy cop.

5

On the ten-dollar bill, Sir John A. Macdonald stares forever somewhere in a purple haze. The dead face of ten bucks. I blink at him. "Why did she leave ten dollars? What the fuck am I going to do with ten dollars? I mean, what can you do with ten bucks?"

"Jeez, Denny . . . "

"You can't do sweet bugger-all with ten bucks! You can't even buy a deck of smokes and a cup of coffee. You can't even buy a decent shit for ten bucks. I owe you ten bucks for picking me up. Here."

"No, it's okay."

"I owe you for gas, Dianne. Take it."

"No, really, forget it."

"Take the goddamn money!" I rattle the bill in her face.

Dianne snaps it from my hand. "Okay, fine. There, I have it. I have your last ten dollars. Now what?"

I am settling into the realization that I have nothing. It's fitting. I spend twenty-eight days drying out, I come home clean and Twyla's gone, my rent's gone, my stereo's gone. I've lost my teeth, I'm losing my eyesight, my sex life is gone. I'm broke. I have no prospects. I have nothing — zilch. What the hell is there to live for?

"This is like, really it. Just when you think you hit bottom, you look around, and shit, you're still falling. The landscape is going by — vertically. When the hell am I going to land? I mean, this has got to be it, right? I mean, how much lower can you go?

"I have this dream. I'm climbing this ladder, and it's in a theatre, backstage in a theatre full of curtains and lights. There's something going on — a play, like Shakespeare or something, and I'm climbing on this ladder to the top, to this catwalk. And suddenly the ladder breaks away, and I just make it to the catwalk, and then the catwalk breaks away, and I grab onto another ladder, and *it* breaks away, and everything I touch starts crumbling, the curtains, the lights . . . "

" . . . and before you land, you wake up. Everybody has that dream, Denny, it's normal."

Dianne finishes — not for me — for herself, just to end the nightmare that admittedly often ends like that. But I can't tell if the wreckage it leaves me in, the shitty mass of skin and bone, is from my liver shutting down or utter terror. Or if I do wake up. All I know is it's out of control.

"I never wake up; I just keep on falling. When the hell am I going to wake up? Hit bottom? What is 'hitting the bottom?' Maybe there is no bottom . . .

"I just want to start over. A clean slate. I can start all over again. With nothing, just my music. This is it, right? Like being reborn. All that shit in the past, everything is gone. I'm clean; I'm clean. I should be thankful, I mean, really, I should be thankful. Hey, I'm alive, I mean, I'm alive. That's important, right? I mean, that's all that really counts, isn't it?

"I should call Mom."

It's two steps to the old black Bakelite phone that hangs from the wall. The reason I still have it is because you can unscrew the microphone cover and attach clips to the wires to render relatively decent high-quality sound. It's for when I want to share my newest work with my agent. I haven't had new work or an agent in fifteen years. But you never know.

The phone, however, is mute as coal.

"The phone is dead. The fucking phone is dead!" I rip the entire machine from the wall and hurl it into the garbage can. I kick the can across the room. "Aaaah!"

"That's it, Denny, let it all out," says Dianne.

"Aaaaah!!!"

I scream at the top of my lungs, but Dianne, rather than cover her ears, hugs me. Holds me.

"It's okay, big guy. It's okay," she says.

I slide through her arms and sit on the floor.

"Well, I think you just hit bottom."

She has dropped the ten-dollar bill. It sits in front of me. I wonder how Twyla missed it, or if she didn't miss it, why she left it. I reach for it but Dianne places her foot on John A. Macdonald's head.

"It's mine," she says.

"I just wanted to look at it awhile."

She lifts her toe.

"Amazing, isn't it. It's paper, or plastic, or whatever it is. It's practically nothing at all and yet, it's everything. People kill for this stuff."

"They also work for it, Denny."

"Do you mind if I keep it?"

"Not at all," she says.

I don't plan on spending it. I plan on keeping around to remind me of hitting bottom.

"I wish there was something I could do, I mean, besides giving you ten dollars."

"I want to get my shit together, Dianne. I want to get my life back together. I want to write music again. I want to make music."

"You will, you will. You've taken the first big step. What did J.K. Rowling say? 'Hitting rock bottom was where I built the foundation for my success.' You're doing it, Denny, and that's good. And there's one thing I want you never to forget — I'll be here. I'll always be here for you, no matter what. Okay?"

Why is she saying these things to me? We haven't exchanged ten words in ten years and yet here she is, holding me.

"Did J. K. Rowling really say that?"

"Apparently — I mean, she *said* it after Harry Potter. She hit bottom *before* Harry Potter."

"Fuck Harry Potter," I pull back. Try to straighten up.

She looks me in the eye. "It's an example. There is always hope."

I'm supposed to look back and acknowledge what she is saying. I glance and turn away. This must be what shame feels like. "I know, I know, I know," I say. But really, I know nothing.

"Good. Just take it easy."

"God, I hate myself. I hate me."

"I love you, Denny. You're a good person."

"If I'm such a good person, why'd Twyla leave?"

"I don't know."

"Not to mention the other dozen or so."

"I don't know."

"At least I knew why Christine left."

"Yes, Christine. But the bottom line is you don't attract very faithful women, Denny."

Maybe they are faithful, just not to me. I meet them at the AA meetings I attend from time to time. They're always more fucked up than I am. Anybody less fucked up knows better.

"And you just haven't been very lucky either," she continues.

"Like you — one guy since grade ten."

"Two guys. I had two guys. Steve was number two."

"Oh, you wicked woman, you."

"I was lucky. You're not."

"It's not luck, Dianne. I got problems; it's me."

"Yes, but you're working on them. You just spent twenty-eight days in rehab. You're doing things about it, that's good. I mean, we all have our problems. I have problems, you have problems. Yours are just peculiar to you, and you're working on them."

"What problems do you have?"

"I have problems, believe me," she says.

"Name one."

"Name one? Just off the top of my head . . . " She pauses briefly here, to scan the great depth and range of choices that sit on top of her head. "Okay, the cottage."

"It's not a cottage, Dianne. It's a cabin."

"You say 'cabin,' I say 'cottage.' You know what I mean."

The cabin is not a problem. It does, however, *have* problems. It festers on the shores of Mahihkan Lake, halfway to the Northwest Territories. It's fed by a small river by the same name. "Mahihkan" — or a word like it — is Cree for wolf. How do I know this? A placemat told me, a feature of the cantina at the Stone's Throw RV Park and Marina filled with area lore, like the monster eel lurking in the 140-foot depths of the lake and how it preys on small children so you better not go in over your head. Also the size of the largest walleye ever caught in the lake and, oh yeah, how it got its name. The Wolf was in charge of fire but agreed with Wolverine not to light any, so they could hide more successfully from hunters. And that's why animals don't have fire. But at certain times, Wolf lights a fire on the far shores of the lake. At any rate, Mom and Dad built the cabin when we were kids. Dad was a terrible carpenter. His motto was "if it's close, it's good." No two joints are square nor do they ever actually meet. The roof sags; the floors heave. It is infested with lower life forms. It needs to be purged. Burnt.

"Either we sell it or pay the back taxes."

"How much are the back taxes?"

"Twenty-two thousand dollars."

"Twenty-two thousand dollars! Building it didn't cost that much!"

"No, but the land's worth at least twice that."

"Twenty-two thousand dollars . . . "

"I know."

Dianne tells me that Mom never paid a dime during the ten years following Dad's death, and Dad never paid more than what he thought he should for the ten years before. Through a maze of mismanagement, neglect and incompetence, this was allowed to drag on for twenty years, give or take a year. Hence the threat of imminent foreclosure. And this, she insists, is a problem.

"So how come you don't buy it?"

"I don't want it, Dennis. There's nothing there but ghosts."

"Okay, *that* is a problem. But on a scale of one to ten it's about a two. I mean, look around, Dianne, read the paper, watch TV — there are problems out there, real problems: wars, poverty, pestilence . . . "

"Pestilence?"

"Bugs! Disease! Plagues! Pandemics! H1N1 viruses that really are killers. The cottage, for God's sake . . . " I try not to dwell on the apocalyptic times we live in. It merely underscores the tiny, trite world that Dianne and her ilk inhabit.

"Alcoholism, drug dependency, addictions — these are problems. I'm an alcoholic. I have to deal with that. I'm a musician who can't get work — that's a problem. I got rent to pay — that's a problem. You understand? What kind of problems do you have? For Christ's sake, something serious."

A brittle pause sits in here. Dianne looks away and down. Her jaw sets. I suddenly sense that we are going to cross from the realm of real estate and taxes into something with a little more oomph. Depth. Perhaps something a little more personal. Dianne has never confided in me about anything before. We have had a very non-intimate sibling relationship. It occurs to me that I don't really know my sister very well. She is a stranger I did not recognize on the street.

"Kirsten," she says.

"Kirsten?"

"Yeah, you know, Kirsten — my daughter, your niece, your godchild . . . "

I nod. I know Kirsten. I have bounced her on my knee. Not lately though.

"She's fifteen going on thirty; she's flunking out of school; she's gone for three or four days at a time; she's running around with some guy with 'Eat Shit' tattooed into his forehead; she tells me to fuck off. She . . . she . . . " Dianne inhales sharply, then exhales in what is almost a sob. "I don't know what to do . . . That's my problem."

"Yes, I can see that. That's a problem." She's got me. It's true. It really is a problem. Being a parent is a problem. Being a parent of a problem child is a problem. I'm so glad I never had kids — or none that I know of. That would be a problem.

"We all have our problems, okay? You do not have the corner on problems."

"Of course not. I sit around all day feeling sorry for myself, and other people have problems too. That's just like me. That's another one of my problems — I think about myself too much. Which is a real joke because there's not much here to think about. I mean, what am I? What have I got? Nothing. So, what's my problem. Christ, am I screwed up. See? See what I'm doing here? I'm turning this whole conversation around to me, to focus on me. Me, myself, and I."

"Yes, you have to figure out a way to change your focus, figure out what it is you want, and once you have that, you have something to shoot for, you have a goal. That's the only way to stay sane," she says.

I have just spent twenty-eight days in rehab and come home with nothing but a box of books, but in less than an hour, Dianne, in one fell swoop, has offered a glimmer of hope.

"A goal. Like something I want."

"Yes."

This has never occurred to me before. What do I want? Besides a drink — what, out there, do I want? "What does Dianne want?" I ask her.

"Me?"

"Yes, what do you want? Like, give me an example."

Hardly missing a beat, she says, "I want my daughter to always have a safe place."

There's a problem here. I can't put my finger on it immediately. It's a perfectly good, non-selfish thing to want — not the kind of thing I would want because it doesn't focus on me. But then, what you want should focus on you, or it's not a want. It's something else.

"You're wanting for someone else. What do *you* want?" I ask.

"That's what I want. If my daughter always has a safe place, then I'll always be at peace."

"That's good. That's very nice," I say. "A nice thing to want. If more people had what they wanted — or even knew what it was, the world would be a better place."

"That is exactly what I believe," says Dianne. "It doesn't even matter if you get what you want, it's just the wanting that matters. It's what keeps you moving."

This is becoming entirely too philosophical. Ontological. Or maybe epistemological. "Ical" words. I can never remember the difference. Why I flunked philosophy.

"What does Kirsten want?"

"She doesn't know what she wants."

"Like me," I say.

"Like you," Dianne agrees.

The little light bulb in my mind flickers on. "I know what I want. I want the truth."

Dianne looks at me for a moment, as though the truth is written all over my face. But, because it's my face, I can't read it.

"That's a good thing to want," she says, tentatively. "About what?"

"About what I want."

"You don't know?"

"Not really, no. Do you?"

"I want health. I want happiness . . . "

She's going to go on with this motherhood list. "Yes, we all want apple pie and ice cream, but I mean, for example, I want to know if I'm any good."

"You're fine, you're great. You're a good person, Denny." She is relieved. This was easy.

"No, I don't mean me — I'm a shit — I mean, my music — is my music any good?"

"You're not a shit. Your music is fine. I like it."

"I didn't ask if you liked it — I asked if it was any good." Is this too small a distinction here? Am I asking the impossible? I'm too close to my music. I've always been too close. I have no idea if it's any good — I know that together with Rick, it was hugely successful and that it was popular and made me a lot of money over the years. "Is my music any good?"

"Denny, how can I separate your work out of what you both did together? How do you unravel Lennon and McCarty? How do you know who did what?"

"It's easy. You just listen."

"Then you're asking the wrong person. I don't know anything about music."

"I trust your opinion. You didn't wake up yesterday. You've been around the block a couple of times. You're an artist. You should know these things — quality, standards . . . "

"I'm a commercial artist. I sell things."

"Yes, but you *think* like an artist. You are creative." And happen to be good at selling. I don't tell her that. I don't want to water down the point.

"You're music is fine — I like it," she says.

"You said that already." The moment someone starts repeating herself means she's avoiding going forward. Spinning her tires.

"I don't know what else to say," she says.

"You can't tell me what you think about my music? Is this so hard? Ask me what I think about your work."

"I don't need to know what you think about my work, and more to the point, I don't want to know," she says, crossing her arms.

I'm not entirely sure why she's being so defensive here. Fear?

"Are you afraid to hear what I have to say? Well, I think it's brilliant! I think it is finely detailed, colourful, appropriate, and concise. I think your work generally represents the concepts you are trying to sell with flare and originality. I think it makes its point with grace and subtleness. I think there is little wonder why people fly you to Toronto and New York to work for them despite the fact that you live out here in the boonies. That's what I think about your work."

"I'm a glorified sign painter, for godsakes!"

"But a very talented one. Now what do you think about my work?"

"Dennis, it takes years to develop craft, style, all that stuff."

"I've been at it for years, Dianne. What are you saying, practise? Is the truth I'm no good?"

"No, no!"

"You haven't even heard me lately," I remind her.

"Yes, right, I haven't."

"I might have improved, you know. I don't just sit around all day abusing myself. I do practise."

"Of course you practise."

"I do spend a large part of my day abusing myself, but I practise. It's my life; it's the only thing I know how to do."

"Of course, of course."

"If I could sell shoes, I'd sell shoes."

"You got to do what you got to do."

"I'd love to be able to do something else, but I just can't."

"You're doing the right thing," she says.

"I would love to be able to quit."

"No, don't do that."

"Why not? I mean, what's the use? You don't think I'm any good anyway."

"I never said that!"

"You said I should practise more. I can't practise anymore, because all I do is practise."

"I never said a word about practise. You did."

She's right. This is all in my head. "Well, then, what's the problem?"

"It takes more than practise; it takes more than it being your life. I mean, you've got to do that, too — but it takes more than that."

"More? There is no more."

"Yes, there is. There's talent, perspective, taste. I have those things and I know how to get paid for them, I just don't know how to use them as a real artist."

"Right. So I know how to use them, I just don't know how to get paid for them."

"No, not quite . . . You don't have the right kind of talent, Denny."

"What?" This is just like my dream, grabbing onto the ladder rung, high among the scaffolding, and it keeps breaking away. My life is a series of illusions and they keep dissolving, breaking off and away.

"I'm being truthful here. You wanted me to tell the truth."

"So, I don't have any talent." I thought talent was the *only* thing I had. I thought I was missing things like luck, good management, discipline, attention to detail — I could make a list — but talent . . .

"The right *kind* of talent," says Dianne, "the right kind of talent is when you can sit down at a desk in grade two and draw a duck, even though you've never drawn a duck before."

"That's talent; you can draw a duck."

"In grade two, yes. Or a horse that looks like a horse."

"So that's the right kind talent."

"Or when you can pick up a guitar or sit at a piano and just play, even though you've never seen a guitar or piano before. You can just sit there and the music pours out of you without trying. That's the right kind of talent, raw talent. You've always had to try."

"I never had a guitar in grade two."

"I know that, Denny. I'm not talking about you personally, just you generally and what talent is." Dianne is furiously twisting the wedding ring on her finger.

"I never had a piano either."

"I know. There was no piano in our house." For the attractive woman that she is, her hands don't fit. She has the hands of a butcher.

"Then how can you say I had no talent?"

"I don't know, Denny!" She's shouting now, flapping her arms like a duck. "It's just an argument — just a discussion. I take it all back. It doesn't mean anything!"

"Einstein couldn't do math in grade two; they would have sent him to the fat-pencil class for Special Ed, if they had such things back then. Shakespeare couldn't even spell his own name!"

"Well there's talent and then there's genius . . . "

"Think if they'd been talented!"

"Okay, okay."

"Don't tell me I've got no talent."

"You're very talented."

"Don't tell me I'm talented either."

"Right, talent has nothing to do with it."

"So, what's the truth then?"

"I have no idea," she says.

The truth is it's impossible to know. The truth is there are some things you just can't know. You never will know. The truth is, what I want more than anything is a drink. The truth is, I will find one too. As soon as Dianne leaves. But she's not quite ready to do that yet.

"It shows signs of being good. It could have been good," she says.

I know that Dianne didn't lug my guitar all the way up here just to discuss whether or not I have/had any talent, or if my music was/is any good, even though she feigns great interest in the subject because it is outside of her — safe and ethereal — but sooner or later, she will segue into her true purpose of being here. When she is good and ready.

"It shows 'signs of being good?' Like what? Like, how do you mean that?" I ask.

"Well, I don't know — it might be good." She has decided to sit on her hands. They were getting out of control. Or maybe she wants to make herself taller.

"It *might* be good? I see. We don't know what good is; we haven't defined it yet."

"Go ahead, you define it, Denny. Define goodness."

The trouble with goodness is that it's relative. One man's good is another man's evil. *One man's word is another man's lie.* Guy Clark. *I don't want to know about evil, I only want to know about love.* Stephen Fearing. I think about open tuning for a moment. I think *talent.* I don't want to go into *goodness.* I don't want to discuss it but Dianne wants me to. *She is not ready yet.*

My guitar sits on the floor, in its case. I've been using it as a foot rest.

"Goodness," I say, toeing my guitar case closer to me, "is like a great big guitar case, and as long as you don't wreck the guitar case, you're good — relatively speaking."

"That's a pretty narrow definition, Denny."

"Well if you wreck the case, you wreck the guitar. I'm talking in metaphors here, Dianne. I'm saying that if you don't harm the outside, you won't harm the innards."

"Oh, so I can bash around your guitar all I want, and that's okay — that's not bad."

"Yes, that's bad. The guitar is just another kind of case — it's a case for the music. That's what's inside."

"The guitar doesn't make the music, you do."

"I make the song; I'm a song case. I carve them out of the air a mouthful at a time."

"But you don't know if they are any good, which is what you are trying to define here."

"Yes, well that's the tricky part, isn't it? Because I'm just making it up, I don't know what's there because it didn't exist before. I don't know if it's good or bad. I'm God when I'm making a song, and even He made bad things — just so he could have balance. If you don't have down, how can you have up? If we only had good, how would we know what evil was?"

"We wouldn't have to, would we?"

"Yes, I'm saying we would. I'm saying bad is necessary. My songs are what you need to see what a good song is. So they're bad, but necessary. And that's what makes them good. If you didn't have disease, there'd be no doctors. First came the outlaws, then came the laws. You got to have the bad in order to have the good."

"So, first came the sinner, and then came the saint?"

"Sure. First came the darkness, then came the light," and as I say this, it is also a kind of revelation to me — like improvising a very cool guitar lick instead of the usual cliché or incoherent mud. It's the kind of thing you can make once, and never repeat. You wonder how you managed it. Real genius can do it again. Then improve, and improve on the improve. "Art, that's what art is."

"What?" says Dianne, not following my inner monologue.

"Making something out of nothing, making music out of the silence."

"Oh, I see," she says, "noise out of the quiet."

"Oh come on, give me some slack. It's more than that. It's not just a roar out of an exhaust pipe." I have jerked Dave into the conversation, as though we've been talking about him all along.

Dianne clears her throat, recognizing this. "That was an interesting metaphor," she says.

"Yeah, well, it just popped out."

"I don't understand why you hated him so much," she says.

"I didn't hate him at all — I probably loved him — I just couldn't stand him. He was a nasty person, a junkie and a thief who stole from everybody he ever made contact with, including Mom and Dad — and probably you, although you would never say so. He'd probably have stolen from me too if he thought I had anything worth taking. And the fact that he was a pimp just blows me away."

"Then why did we all feel so shitty, so incredibly shitty when he died? How come you went completely bananas, howling at the moon till the police came and took you away? How come whenever I see a motorcycle come rising over a hill, I get this little swell in the pit of my stomach, and I hope against all hope that somehow, impossibly, it could be him? How come? And I have this stupid box of ashes that prove he's dead, and still I wait."

She turns away, having admitted something that neither of us is keen to hear — maybe having something to do with guilt, a feeling that we share some kind of responsibility for

Dave ending up the way he did. But I don't say anything. I think her questions are rhetorical anyway. But it does occur to me why she wants to sell the cottage. Twenty-two thousand dollars is half of one of the cars in her garage. So it's not really the money, the back taxes. It's more than that.

"So that's why you want to sell the cottage."

"No . . . Yes."

"He liked to party hearty."

"Yes."

"You were right, you know, to kick him out. I mean, he was probably wrecking the place — even more than it was already wrecked."

"Yes, but I didn't mean for him to kill himself."

"You can't take responsibility for that anymore than I can. Besides, he hadn't left, you know. The accident report is pretty clear about the direction he was heading, and it wasn't south. He must have been heading back up to the place."

"He's dead, Denny, dead, dead, dead. And you're *not*. Don't you get it?"

"What am I supposed to get? Am I supposed to feel lucky? I've hit bottom, you know. When you hit bottom, you bounce. So this is what I'm doing now — on the bottom, bouncing."

"You'll bounce back. That's what life is about."

"Yeah, right. The only problem is that you never bounce quite as high. Eventually, you just sort of lie there."

"I wish you didn't feel so sorry for yourself all the time."

"I wish I didn't too."

I had forgotten how sweet she really is and how undeserving for her to have a brother like me. I'm thinking this without self-pity. It is a matter of fact. Anyone looking in from the outside would think the same thing. *That poor girl has such a jerk for a brother,* is what they'd say. And of course they'd be right. Let me try to be nice to her, to not alienate her beyond how alien we already are with each other. *She's trying to reach out, Denny,* I tell myself. *Humour her.*

"You see how complicated it gets?" This isn't so much a question as it is me trying to be rational. Trying to dig myself out of this stupid hole.

"Yes, of course, I see how hard it is."

"And don't agree with me just to raise my self-esteem."

"I'm sorry."

"And don't apologize. I'm just trying to explain how impossible it is. I just can't do it."

"*Won't* do it," she corrects.

"Go ahead, sure — blame the victim!"

"You're doing what you're doing to *yourself.* You are your own victim."

"I rest my case, again."

I sense that Dianne and I are at a stalemate, and if I don't do something pretty quickly, Dianne is going to up and away, taking her Saab with her all the way back to her mansion on the east side. And we will likely never see each other again.

"Did you read the letter?" I ask.

"You told me not to read it. Unless something happened to you. Nothing happened to you. I didn't read it."

She has rehearsed this response. I can tell. It was too quick and too ready. I'll try another tack.

"If something happened to you, would you want me to do something for you?"

"Nothing is going to happen to me."

"Well, you never know, eh? I mean, you just might flop over and die right here in front of me. Aneurism. *Phht!* Gone. Then what? It could happen you know. People die all the time. What's going to happen to Kirsten? Who's going to look out for her?"

"She has a father, Dennis. Steven will look out for her."

"So what if something happens to both of you?"

"You want to look out for Kirsten?"

"I'm her godfather."

"Sure, fine. If something happens to me *and* Steve, you can look out for Kirsten. And Mom."

"Both of them?"

"Well, I'm looking after both of them now. If I'm gone, they'd *both* need looking after, right?"

"That's a lot of responsibility — responsibilities, plural. I don't have rent; I don't have an apartment. Where would we live?"

Dianne suddenly springs to her feet, grabbing the plastic garbage bag. "I'm tired of playing with you. I'm going. This is nuts."

"Sure, ask me to take care of Kirsten and Mom, and I don't even have a place to stay."

"You want a place to stay, stay on the street. Goodbye!" she says, opening the door and stepping into the hallway.

You say hello, I say goodbye, hello, goodbye. "Dianne, the letter was from Dave!" I don't exactly shout this because I know I don't need to. I know it will stop her even if she just *thinks* she heard me.

She re-enters through the door and stands in the doorway holding the green garbage bag, making her look like some sort of undecided eco-Santa all dressed in green. "What did it say?"

"You should have read it."

"What did it say?" she repeats, articulating a little more carefully.

"When I was in Cape Breton and Dave was in jail, what happened to you?"

"What do you mean?"

"In Kelowna — you were in Kelowna apparently and Dave said he was sorry for what happened there and everything else. What happened?"

"I was working in a restaurant."

"And?"

"You don't want to know."

"No? Who's Jimmy Matheson?"

"Who?"

"Jimmy Matheson, the guy who's supposed to be looking for you."

"I don't know."

"You don't know?

"No. I've never heard the name before."

"You're not going to tell me."

"I don't know!"

"Oh." This puts everything into a different light. She really doesn't know. I guess that settles that. I turn from Dianne and walk to my bed where I think for a second about crawling under the blankets and never getting up. Instead, I get on my knees and reach beneath.

"What's the matter?" she says.

"Nothing." It's where I keep my large duffel bag. I drag it from under my bed and begin collecting whatever is lying around and throwing it inside. Dianne remains standing at the door.

"What are you doing?" she asks.

"What does it look like? I'm packing."

"Why are you packing?"

"Dianne, I don't have my rent. It's overdue. I'm moving out before I'm thrown out."

"Where are you going to go?"

"Didn't you just mention that the street would be a pretty good location for me? I'll find a nice bridge to sleep under."

"I was just kidding," she says.

"Well, don't kid. Lies I can tolerate, but I hate kidding."

"You could stay at my place."

"Are you kidding me?"

"You said not to kid."

"I don't think so, Dianne." Not for ten seconds could I be comfortable with her and Steve and Kirsten and Mom or a single square foot of their mansion including its pool and Jacuzzi flanked by the Saab and its two shiny companions in the three-car garage.

"I mean, until you find a bridge."

"You're kidding again, aren't you."

"Teasing. Teasing is different from kidding. What about the cottage?"

This stops me. I've been attempting to stuff an old wooden tennis racket into the duffle bag. The racket wouldn't get fifty cents at Value Village. There are things you should just throw out. I study the racket. It actually has gut strings.

"I don't want to stay at the cottage, I mean, it's for sale, isn't it? What if someone wants to buy it?"

"We'll take down the For Sale sign."

I realize I have never in my life played tennis, that this racket must have belonged to someone else. There is a name written on the handle. *Billy Jean Moffitt*, it says. I don't remember anyone by that name, which doesn't mean much.

"Didn't you say they're too many ghosts?" I say.

"We'll exorcise them," she says.

"*We?*"

"Yeah. You and me. We can be together for a while. Go fishing. Play cards. Fly around the room."

Going fishing and playing cards were the primary activities of cottage life in those three or four years filled with gilt-edged memories. Missing are the mosquitoes, the rain, the noisy neighbours, the cuts and bruises, plus the constant threat of fires and bears. But flying around the room. That was something else altogether. "Fly around the room?"

"You remember," she says.

"Of course, yes, I remember. That was very bizarre."

"Yes, it was," she says. "Me and Dave, up there, flying around the room. A couple of cherubs. I mean, that's impossible, you know. It must have been like a group dream or something."

"I don't think so."

"And you made us promise not to tell anyone," says Dianne. "Not now, not ever . . . "

And together we both say, "Never."

"I wonder why I did that?" If I had a reason, I can no longer remember what it was. Maybe fear of ridicule. Maybe guilt.

"I don't know. I don't know why we didn't tell the whole world. But it must have made sense for us to make it our secret. And it only happened that once," says Dianne. "And we can do something with Dave's ashes."

"Yeah, we can do that — bury the pimp."

"Maybe fly around the room," says Dianne.

94

6

The jowly cop is busy with paperwork while Harold fidgets in the back seat of the black SUV. The nerdy cop has climbed aboard Harold's rig and returns holding a wide-mouthed bottle that once held lemon tea.

"What's this, Harold?" He holds up the bottle.

Harold thinks for a moment. It looks like tea, but he knows that the cop probably knows it's not, and if he pretends that it is, the cop might ask him to take a swig, just to prove it. Harold knows that some people actually drink their urine — but they are crazy people, like Adolf Hitler. And there were those miners stuck in the bottom of that coal mine with nothing to drink — they were really desperate, though.

"It's my piss," says Harold.

"You always pee in a bottle?"

Harold now thinks maybe he should make a crack, like, "Yeah, I'm savin' it for something . . . " He can't think of what he might be saving it for, and that it probably wouldn't go over too well anyway, so he just nods and says, "Sometimes."

"You do this while you're driving?" asks the nerdy cop.

Admitting that he does would be pleading guilty to *Dangerous Operation of a Motor Vehicle*, and a guaranteed way of getting his licence suspended, whereas *Failure to Stop at the Scene of an Accident* — especially if somebody got killed — would just get you sent to jail. Shit, he is in so much trouble. He wishes he had a lawyer now or somebody to tell him what the safest thing to say is. Maybe his grandson will be a lawyer. That's not much help to him now though. The little prick can't even finish high school. Harold didn't finish high school either. But times were different then. Maybe a little white lie will do the trick. "You can't piss and drive," he says.

"So how'd the urine get into the bottle, Harold?" asks Jowly.

"I put it there. There was all kinds of traffic when I pulled over and I didn't want to get charged with indecent exposure, so I did it into the bottle." *And you can't prove otherwise,* he thought. It was amazing how quick and easy the lie came.

"Where'd you stop?" asks Nerdy.

Suddenly, Harold doesn't feel so smug about the ease of his lie. It flusters him. Where did he stop? Where *would* he have stopped — if he had stopped? How could they check? *Could* they check? "How can I remember where I stopped?' he says.

"Well, was it ten minutes ago, twenty? . . . The bottle's still warm, Harold."

Oh, shit, thinks Harold. *I'm fucked.*

Sepia

7

It's a long drive up here past galleons of forest that float off the highway, their green sails crowding the roadside. *Hiding, your home and native land/Hiding in a sheepskin glove.* And somewhere along the way our dear brother did himself in, caught up under the wheels of gravel truck. The idiot pimp. Mind you, he had a little help from my bottle of gin. Maybe without that, he'd still be around.

Just before dark, we turn off the main highway onto the secondary road leading to Mahihkan Lake. Everything looks as it always has with the rolling green through woods, rock, and water, until we reach the Mahihkan Village fork. Suddenly, blackened stands of naked spruce stand over charcoaled earth. It looks like an armada of masts in an endless black harbour. Inexplicable islands of green stand in its midst. We angle down a back road towards the cabin.

"Did you know about this?" I ask.

"Yes," says Dianne. "Apparently a few cottages in The Cove went up in smoke too. Not ours, of course. Real Point seems to have been spared. They think it was set on purpose, but naturally some of the insurance companies insist it was an 'act of God'."

"I take it there's no insurance against an 'act of God'."

"Well there is, if you pay for it. But if it's arson, it's easier to make a claim."

"Live and learn," I say.

Dianne laughs. I'm not sure what the joke is.

The Lake is always a good place to be at night when you can almost imagine life before the onslaught of humanity that combed then crammed every corner of the green earth, and lights were not flickering in cabins on the far shore, and an orange sodium glow was not rising from the Stone's Throw RV Park and Marina. But there it is, along with the rest of the village. It should be called Ennisville because Bob Ennis owns most of it, but it is actually called "The Resort Village of Mahihkan Lake." "For Sale" signs have hung on most of the commercial property for as long as I can remember, so long they're faded, washed out, and not a few are full of bullet holes, but no one is buying. Too pricey.

Bob Ennis is the mayor of Mahihkan Lake as well as the owner-slash-manager of the Stone's Throw. He took it over when his dad died about twenty years ago. His dad was mayor, too. Bob took over that as well and he's been unchallenged since. Bob is grooming his son to be the next in line because that is the way it is meant to be, kind of like the Divine Right of Kings. He — or some other family member — runs some aspect of the business; however, Bob oversees it all, tightwad asshole that he is. But nobody will tell him so because he is the only store within eighty kilometres, sells the only gas, tires and lubricants for all manner of vehicles, including domestic and foreign cars, has the only bar, and runs the sole septic tank service within the same distance. In short, he controls everything you need at the lake. To be on the wrong side of Bob is not a good plan.

The lake is shaped like a molar. The village is on the high ground between the two roots — arms of the lake. Real Point, where we are, is directly north of the village about a kilometre across the northern arm. The lake blends in with the sky at night, except for the reflection of the Stone's Throw, but it's close enough to smell the cool damp of it. Of course it could be just the rain — not a hard rain really, just enough to make things miserable.

The best thing you can say about the cabin is that it's still standing and remarkably untouched by the fire. The roof is still tight despite its sag. Nothing has changed inside or out for forty-five years, or nothing obvious. The alterations that did occur took so long that they were impossible to notice. When were those curtains put up? Mom probably found them at a garage sale thirty-five years ago. What covered the windows before them? No one would remember, not even Dianne. The couch has been here since day one. It once sat in the living room at the "ha-house" as Dave called it before he moved it into the "ga-garage." From there, it found its way out here.

If this couch had eyes . . .

Today it would have seen Dianne haul in her sleeping bag, a small suitcase, and a provision-packed cooler. It would have seen me with most of my earthly possessions tucked in a backpack, along with Mr. Martin and three bottles of distilled essence of the juniper berry — gin. We also sweep the mouse turds and cobwebs from the counters, cupboards, and the inevitable disaster area beneath the sink, where God knows what critters have lived and died. Then we light a fire and hope the old stove doesn't explode. On it sits a battered kettle with bits of wire engaged in the dubious task of attaching the handle to its body. Dianne fills it with water for her tea.

There are no real signs of Dave having spent a lot of time here — a few bottles, some grease or oil stains in the middle of the front stoop where he must have dismantled something on his bike to inspect or repair. But everything else is pretty well folded and put away. I have to revise some of my earlier trepidations about him wrecking the place.

"Ka-ka-keeping your shop ka-ka-clean, is part of the job," he used to say.

We have set Dave in the middle of the room, on the ancient yellowed floor — the splintering, don't-just-wear-socks, tongue-and-groove fir. He occupies a ceramic urn disguised as cookie jar. I make this observation and Dianne tells me it *is* a cookie jar.

"It's appropriate," she says, "Dave loved cookies. He was a regular Cookie Monster."

I don't want to get into a discussion describing the type of monster Dave may or may not have been but admit the jar is an improvement over the cardboard box he apparently arrived in from the crematorium. Dave is the centrepiece, the real reason for our coming here. We haven't decided exactly what we're going to do yet — how we're going to dispose of the ashes, whether we'll dump him in the lake or climb one of the hills and send him on the wind, but it'll come up sooner or later.

Right now we're trying to get the water going. This is a ritual at the cabin. In the spitting rain where the wind hisses like an old black cat, we shiver above the hole that is the well beside the small pump house. The pump whirrs and sucks, but builds no pressure. Dianne holds the flashlight while I sort through the rusted and worn remnants of Dad's old tools. I clang and bang and swear, all sound and fury indicating I'm not much good at this.

As a child, Dave was the one who "volunteered" to shinny down the well ladder to inspect the foot valve, and clear away the slimy smothering crap. The pump is ancient but it seems to run. We've spent two hours priming it, but still no water. One of us, likely me, is going to have to climb down to check the valve. I say *likely* me because you never know when Dianne will want to take charge, and assert her anything-you-can-do-I-can-do-better attitude. This may once have stood between us as badge of her feminism but I'm sure it's degenerated into ageism, which is fine with me. Damned if I want to crawl down there.

"We're going to have to go down," I say.

"I'll go," she says.

"Don't be silly," I protest, albeit falsely.

"Denny, I'm smaller, lighter and stronger — and used to cleaning things."

I'm happy she doesn't mention the age difference — she's a very young forty-five while I'm an ancient fifty. We tie a rope around her waist. She stuffs the flashlight into her mouth and in the half-light, takes on the guise of a Cyclops. She begins the descent. I let the rope out slowly. It is slick, and although the well is only about twelve feet deep, it seems bottomless.

Suddenly, Dianne screams, "Aaah!" She is not in terror though — more like muffled disgust. But then she has a flashlight in her mouth.

"What!" I yell, almost losing grip of the rope.

The light is now flitting back and forth, waving about in her hand. She's standing a couple of feet of water. "There's a body down here!"

"What?" I strain to see what Dianne has obviously encountered — a mouldy, bloated, half-rotted corpse, its empty eye sockets and immense grin grimacing back at her.

"It's a rat!" she says.

I'm at once relieved and disgusted. "Oh," I say.

"Or maybe a mouse," she corrects.

"Forget the mouse! Unclog the foot valve!"

She is soon back at the surface, untying the rope from her waist.

"So where's the dead mouse?" I ask.

"I wasn't going to touch that thing," she says. "Where was I going to put it? In my pocket?"

"I would have thrown you down a bag."

"Now he tells me."

"Dianne, we can't leave a dead mouse rotting in the well water. We use that water."

"We don't drink it," she says.

"No, but we wash with it," I say.

After attaching a soup ladle to the end of a fishing rod line and unsuccessfully trying to snag-scoop the tiny corpse, I tie a rope around *my* waist and go down with a plastic bag to bring the critter up. Dianne manages to lower and raise me without misshaping our egos too badly.

The pump miraculously begins spitting water and sludge through the line which we then connect, affording us water to the toilet and kitchen sink. I pour the better part of cup of bleach into the hole and hope for the best — that any well-dwelling organisms are now also corpses. I hope none of them are mice, and that they are not what plugged up the foot valve in the first place.

The fire we lit earlier has warmed the place and we're getting comfortable.

I'm noodling on my guitar. I have a glass of clear liquid, gin, on the small coffee table in front of me. I've fallen off the wagon already. I haven't actually *fallen* off — I've *jumped* off. I hate wagons. Always have. They are things you just drag along behind you.

Dianne is sitting on the couch, drinking tea and knitting. She is telling a story — highlights of life with Dad and Dave after I'd left home. I guess that's what you do at a wake — tell stories about the dead. And why not, that's why we're here.

"So I'm getting carsick every twenty minutes, and making Dad pull over so I can puke outside, and it's taking us forever to get there. What's worse is that we're taking two nuns with us . . . "

"Wait a minute — nuns? As in sisters, as in brides of God?"

" . . . complete with their little grey skirts and white blouses — this is a very modern congregation of nuns — the Grey Nuns — they do hospitals and that sort of thing, and they wear their own clothes, but it's kind of drab — Mennonitey — anyway, they want to see the Pope too, and they are praying the whole way, out loud, saying Rosaries, in French . . . "

"In French?"

"With Mom."

"Mom doesn't know French."

"Mom was taught by French nuns till she was thirteen." She sips her tea.

"I didn't know that."

"There's lots you don't know, Denny."

She keeps saying that — in the vague shape of a threat — but continues.

"So, by now it's getting dark and we've got a long way to go yet. We pull into this service station and there's a motel around the back where we should really spend the night, but Dad wants to 'push on'. He gets Gravol for me, to settle my stomach, fills the tank with gas, and goes to pay for it. I've gone to the bathroom (God, the bathroom is another story), so I'm standing right there by the cash register and the cashier says this really strange thing: she says, 'Watch out for the rabbits.'"

"'Watch out for the rabbits.'" If our family had a totem, it would be the rabbit — not for its fecundity, but for how it jumps. To conclusions.

"Yes. Anyway, we take off. We drive and drive . . . "

"On stolen tires."

"What?"

"There's lots you don't know either, Dianne."

"Whatever. This is my story. The road isn't even paved anymore; we're in the middle of nowhere; it's dark. I'm in the front between Mom and Dad. They're not fighting because of the nuns in back seat — but you can feel the tension. They are both staring straight ahead. I'm in the back between the two nuns. All of a sudden, there's this *thump*. Then another, then another. It's like drum beats, I swear. I look and there is a this sea of rabbits — hundreds of them — thousands of pink eyes dancing in the headlights, bouncing all over the road, off the car, and Dad is ploughing through them like they're snow. Dad's mouth is open; his eyes are like saucers. He turns the windshield wipers on to wipe away the rabbits . . . " Dianne stops. She too is looking through the windshield at the wipers. Then she shakes her head. "And then they're gone. But everybody is wide awake, wondering what the hell just happened. The nuns start saying the rosary again. They're French: *Je vous salut Marie pleine de grace* . . . "

"Where'd you learn French?"

"No, wait," she says.

I'm going to have to wait to find out where she learned French. Our childhood was filled with nuns and priests, but none of them were French. Dianne was not taught by French nuns like our mother. Why were they travelling with two French nuns?

"France French or Quebec French?"

"Belgian, Denny."

"Belgian! Like the horses?"

"Denny, can I finish my story? Why are you stuck on the nuns?" She slops some of her tea onto the floor.

"Sorry," I say.

"So. We finally get to another service station town. We haven't stopped for nothing . . . for *anything*," she corrects herself. "We all get out and the car is covered in blood. There are little bits of rabbit stuck into the grill: bunny tails, feet, ears. 'Oh,' says the guy filling the tank. 'I see you hit the rabbits.' 'Yeah,' says Dad. 'We hit the rabbits,' like this happens all the time. 'You better wash your car,' the guy says. 'They can plug things up, cause you all kinds of grief.' 'I don't have time,' says Dad. 'We're going to see the Pope.' 'Oh,' says the guy. 'Everybody's going to see the Pope.'"

"Which is where, Belgium?"

"Fort Simpson, Denny."

"Way up there?"

"In the Northwest Territories, yes. And we're on our way there. We keep driving. It's hot in the car. It starts to smell. Cooked hare — rare, well done. Everybody's getting nauseous. I start throwing up again. The nuns have stopped praying, they're gasping. We open the windows, but the dust is unbelievable. We close the windows. Then the engine starts overheating and we have to stop. The radiator is all blocked up with dead rabbit bits. Dad is trying to pick away at it, and all the bugs in northern Alberta find us. Black flies, mosquitoes, horse flies . . . "

"Pestilence! This is all very biblical, Dianne."

"The nuns go crazy. They jog up and down the road trying to outrun the bugs. Finally, a car stops. They hitch a ride. They're gone. We get back in our car; we drive a few more miles, and the engine overheats. And Dad stops every few kilometres, gets out of the car and reloads the radiator with water. Then is starts raining and getting foggy and it's freezing cold — it's the middle of September, and we pitch a tent some place in the dark in the rain. It was the most miserable thing you can imagine. And the Pope never showed up. Dad says, 'If God wanted us to see the Pope, He wouldn't have sent the rabbits.'"

She laughs at the punchline. It doesn't strike me as very funny; it doesn't strike me as very true either. It makes you wonder how the imagination works building a convenient, or inconvenient, memory to explain something. Disguise something. Hide something. I wonder what?

"So you never got to see him?"

"Well, we would have but no, he never arrived. He never made it to Fort Simpson. He got fogged in, or out. I don't know, but he went to Yellowknife instead. And we drove back home. No rabbits. Just a long boring drive."

"So, no rabbits, eh?"

"Not on the way back, no, not one."

"Doesn't sound very plausible to me," I say.

"You don't believe me?"

"You were, what, eight years old?"

"Nine."

"I think you made it up to hide something."

"Like what?"

"I don't know — why do people make up stories?"

"I didn't make it up. It actually happened."

"Along with two Belgian nuns — where'd they come from? I mean, that you be travelling with them."

"How should I know? I was nine years old."

"See?"

"What?"

"It's just not very believable."

"No more or less believable than flying around the room. I suppose that never happened either."

"Not the way you remember it, no."

"Why not? We were all there."

"Yeah, but I just watched."

"You flew, too."

"No, Dianne, I didn't. I couldn't. It was something special between you and Dave."

This is when she fires her cup of tea at me. It catches me in the jaw.

8

Harold has never in his life spoken to a lawyer. He didn't know they could be so young, younger even than the doctor who prescribed his piss pills. He'd feel more comfortable with somebody closer to his age, even half his age. Not only is his lawyer young, she's a girl. She looks like she should still be in high school. He knows that times are changing and that women do pretty well everything that men do now, even those things that were once the exclusive domains of the male gender, hings like lawyering, and yes, trucking. He supposes they're not having kids, how could they? Who'd look after them? When he began driving truck, there was no such thing as a woman driver. Now they're all over the place, and not just spouses of male drivers, but gals who solo long hauls. And some of them don't even look like men. He's heard stories of all kinds about these women drivers. They frighten him. Well, maybe not exactly fill him with fear, but they definitely make him uncomfortable.

The schoolgirl lawyer has advised him to plead guilty to a lesser charge so that he's less likely to go to jail.

"*Less* likely?"

"Well, yes. It's still a possibility," she says.

All this for pissing in a bottle — something he's been doing for years.

On top of all this, the judge is a woman too. She, at least, is nearer his age. She reminds Harold of his wife — his ex-wife who left him after twenty-five years of marriage. He didn't understand why. Harold never hit her, never screwed around. Yes, he yelled sometimes and locked her in the basement once just after their seventh anniversary. But that was a long time ago and it was just to teach her a lesson about something or other that must have been pretty important but now he can't remember what. He doubts if she learned it though, whatever it was, she had a strong mind, a will of her own. She took everything, both kids, the house, the good car — he got stuck with the beater — and froze the bank account till some judge made sure every dime he ever earned was split right down the middle. The kids don't talk to him any more, not that he cares — they are just like their mother — but he does get along with his book-reading grandson. He wonders if his grandson will visit him in jail. It's the only family that means anything to him.

Harold didn't realize he had so little till it was all divvied up. He had to move into an apartment where scowling neighbours and their kids howl and thump on the walls and ceiling twenty-four seven. It's enough to drive you crazy. He was left with the camper, which Reta always hated — there were too damn many bugs for her. She wasn't interested in his toys, he snow mobile, the canoe, his fishing gear, guns, and tools. He sold the camper because it never got used anymore, a damn shame too. Reta left him his rig too, of course, which was worth something then. Except now this woman judge is about to take that away too by suspending his license.

She asks if he has anything to say in his defence, and Harold thinks he has plenty to say — beginning with what is he doing here? He's been driving truck for longer than his lawyer has been on the planet and never had so much as a speeding ticket; he's been peeing in bottles almost as long and never had anything resembling a close call because of it, either. He would also like to know how he can get the blame for a biker that somehow came up behind him, and as near as he can figure out, threw himself under the rig when he was halfway past. And what about the bus? Even if there weren't any scratches on that bus, the backdraft from it could have knocked the biker his way, and how was he to know? Peeing in a bottle had nothing to do with the biker's death. He didn't stop because he didn't know anything had happened. That's what he thinks he should say. Instead he coughs and says, "No, your Honour."

He wonders why the judge seems to be studying him, as if she is still waiting for him to say more. He opens his mouth slightly trying to find shape for words, but nothing comes. He looks about the courtroom for support from somewhere. But there is none.

Fuck, thinks Harold, *now what am I going to do?*

The judge has suspended his licence — *regretfully* — she said. "I know it affects your livelihood . . . "

Wrong, thinks Harold. *It does not* affect *my livelihood — it* is *my livelihood.* But he could probably survive for six months doing this and that, move into the cabin, live off the land, if it wasn't going to cost him damn near five thousand dollars in fines and relicensing. He hasn't even thought about insurance yet. He would have to sell everything he owns, what do they call that? *Liquefy his assets*. Yeah. That's what he will have to do. Sell the quad, the snowmobile (and he just put a new track on it last spring). Hell would freeze over before he sold the cabin, even though it's worth shit. The guns? No, maybe he can get six Gs for the quad and snow machine, or close — they are six or seven years old. Wait, the quad is ten years old. He bought it on his grandson's sixth birthday — took him quading. Shit. He'll be lucky to get a grand for it. Maybe he will have to sell his guns. His guns and the canoe. The canoe is a gem. A fifteen-foot Prospector. Kevlar, light as air. It's worth twenty-five hundred all by itself. No, he's not going to sell the canoe. He'll do himself in before he sells the canoe. And maybe that's not such a bad idea, doing himself in. What the fuck good is he anyway? Can't even drive his fuckin' truck. Who would miss him? No one. Probably not even his grandson.

The idea appeals. Put the canoe in the water, head up the Mahihkan to the cabin and vanish. Who'd know? That'd fuck 'em up. Fuck 'em all.

9

It's not like it was a big mess to clean up, or that the cup did any damage to my jaw, but I did resent that some of the tea splashed onto Mr. Martin, trickling down into his sound hole. It would not be the first time liquid found a way inside. I'm just hoping tea is not the magic formula for dissolving the glue that holds him together.

Still, it was a lousy way to end a good day.

Dianne stormed off to bed while I tiptoed around trying to clean up a bit. Eco-plumbing didn't exist when this place was built and Dad would never have thought to do anything beyond dig a hole filled with rocks for the "grey" water anyway. The fact that it probably leaches back into the well never occurred to him. Or if it did, he didn't care. Thank goodness they made him put in a septic tank for the toilet, which has its own little building opposite the well-side of the cabin. At any rate, I'm thinking of this when I rinse out the dishcloth I've used to mop up Mr. Martin. I play a few tentative chords — those ninths halfway down the neck sound good right now — but I put him in his plush black coffin for the night.

The main kitchen/living area is one big room. The front door faces more or less south to the lake and is set in the centre of the wall. The back door is directly across from it facing the woods and meandering rock-infested trail to the corduroyed sub-division road, still a half kilometre from the paved highway. You've got to want to come here to get here — and then you have to know the way. It's impossible to give directions.

I'd like to go for a bit of a stroll to cool off. The stove has rendered the cabin into a sauna but it's still spitting rain and there would not be much point in stumbling around in the dark. I open the door and stare into the night. I wonder if I had flung the little dead mouse far enough into the bush to put it out of sight.

I step outside, holding the door open. The cool drizzle on my face contrasts the heat radiating on my back from the wood stove behind. The stove sits ten feet from the door at the head of a wide passageway which is flanked on either side by bedrooms. Dianne is in "her" bedroom where she is silent, silent, silent. Flying around the room. What *was* that, really?

The bedroom walls do not go to the ceiling nor do they have doors; curtains, old, living-room window drapes hang there instead, the colour of weak tea with cream, festooned with plate-sized fuchsias. Astonishingly ugly.

I close the door and turn to pull back the curtain to her room. She lies on her side, her back to me. I know she is not sleeping because Dianne does not sleep on her side. She sleeps either flat on her stomach or flat on her back. Some things you don't forget.

"Dianne?"

"Fuck off," she says.

"All right . . . G'night then . . . I'm sorry." I am too. I'm wondering about these little bubbles I'm bursting.

I'm wondering who Jimmy Matheson is. I'm wondering why she doesn't know. I'm wondering why she didn't read the letter. You don't do that unless you don't want to face something, which means she had a very good idea of what was in it. She didn't need to read it.

I've dragged along Mr. Guzman's *Reflexiones* book. It is a handsome little book. I've grown attached to it somehow. I like its size and its taupe colour, its embossed silver lettering. It stands for the possibility of change, never mind that I can't read it. However, I bought a small Spanish-English dictionary in case I should want to. So far, I've learned that *"diarias"* means "daily." There is a *reflexione* for every day of the year.

I turn to today, 23 de Agosto. I take it that's the twenty-third of August. *"Llevar el Mensaje al Hogars"* is the title of today's reflection. My trusty dictionary informs me that it literally means "To Take the Message Home." I wonder what the message is, and who will do the taking. I know where home is. It's here, for now. Maybe till Dianne sells it. It will be good to get away from my loft above the paint shop. If the manager-slash-landlord wasn't such a decent sort, I probably would have weaseled my way without rent for another year or so. He must have had a thing for musicians; the half-baked night-watchman gig was really his way of being a patron of the arts. I just couldn't take advantage of him anymore. He probably went to church on Sundays. I left him all my ancient gear and a message: "This stuff is supposed to be worth a fortune on eBay. I hope it helps cover my last three months' rent."

The wind is picking up. The black rain is lashing against the windows.

I go to bed.

Dianne and I are maybe ten feet apart. On different planets. I fall asleep. I dream of swimming mice.

Dianne is not around when I get up. The car is gone so I'm fairly certain I've been abandoned. It's still pissing rain and there are whitecaps on the lake. It could be a long day. Dave has been moved from the centre of the floor to a shelf beside the stove. The cookie jar looks inviting, like you want to reach in and grab an Oreo.

Then I notice her knitting is still where she left it on the couch last night; her suitcase lies sprawled open at the foot of her bed. I stop worrying about being stranded. I stop feeling guilty. I'm the one with the teacup imprinted on my jaw — figuratively, that is. There is merely a vague hint of a bruise where it hit. Still, it was a disconcerting display of violence.

Beside her knitting sits a trade magazine she has dragged along, *In Dezine.* I leaf through it. Dianne is listed as a contributing editor. I wonder if she contributed to the cute misspelling of mag's title. I see her byline on an article called "Incorporating Trends in Bedroom Design." I read to discover that what's old is new again, that yesteryear's lace is in vogue once more. Is this the lesson for *hogar* — for home? Somehow, I am not reassured.

Although the leaves had not yet turned, late August this far north can quickly chill a place, so I set about to fill the ancient stove with a few sticks of brittle wood that lie in the bottom of the woodbin against the back wall. I hope to get a blaze going to heat some water as well, and get some coffee into me before the familiar itch begins for gin.

The fire is leaping soon enough behind the grate and the isinglass flickers its mesmerizing dance while the water in the kettle begins to shimmy with life. On the counter, I balance a cone filter holder on top of an old Thermos bottle, place a filter in it, and fill it with coffee. When the water is a rolling boil, I take the kettle to the counter and pour the water into the filter while steadying it with my left hand.

This is when the handle lets loose.

The lid explodes and the entire contents of the kettle pour across my hand and onto my leg.

I turn to the sink, turn on the tap and let cold well water — the mousey stew — flow over my hand. It is all I can do to stand there while the pain forces its way through my body.

I'm wondering if there's ice in the freezer and maybe sticking my hand in a bowl of it. You're supposed to do this to diminish the heat, to stop your flesh from cooking. It's my left hand, my chording hand, the back of it — I still have finger prints. *This was how it must have felt for Dave — only ten times worse because it was his face too,* is my first thought. My upper thigh does not hurt nearly as much as my hand. It looks like a lobster claw. I'm feeling sorry for all those lobsters I have tossed into boiling water. This would not be a good way to die, although you would not live long. Would you? People have survived serious burns. Look at Dave. Django Reinhardt lost the use of two fingers from a burn. All I have is a scalded hand.

Either the pain is beginning to subside or I am getting used to it. I turn the water off and step back from the sink. Instantly, the searing heat returns. I turn the tap back on and let the cool water run over it again. I listen to the pump kick in. At the same time, I also hear Dianne pull into the back. I look at Dave over on the counter, hiding in the cookie jar. "She's back," I say. Dave does not answer.

Dianne kicks open the screen door, bulging plastic grocery bags hanging from each hand.

"I got you a gig!" she announces, "at the Stone's Throw Cantina." She is wearing a big grin.

"Thank you," I say. Then I hold up my claw for a moment.

Her eyes widen. She drops the bags on the table. "Did you do that on purpose?" she asks.

10

His grandson has agreed to drive Harold to a place where he can launch the canoe. This service will cost him though — the use of the beater while his licence is suspended. If he doesn't get it back, it'll be no great loss. It's a vintage Fiesta — his wife got the LTD after the divorce. She's since sold it, and now owns a Camry Hybrid. She always thought she was hoity-toity. Now she's got the car to prove it. No big deal, though. He could not give a shit.

Harold and his grandson have hoisted the Prospector on top of the Fiesta and tied it down good and tight. It's not going anywhere without their permission. He figures he'll launch it near the bridge at the Little Mahihkan which eventually hooks up with the Big Mahihkan and flows into the lake of the same name. There's never anybody around, and if there is, he can just wait till they're gone. He doesn't want anyone watching while he shoves off and tries to clamber aboard. He knows it's going to be none too graceful. It's been a long time since he's paddled a canoe, and even longer since he's paddled solo.

When he was first married, he and Reta used to go out in the evening after the wind died down. They'd paddle to a quiet spot, then just drift awhile, untangle their fishing gear and cast into the shallows, not caring if they caught anything. A good thing, too, for as much as Reta enjoyed tossing out a line, she hated fish, and it was up to Harold to gut, fillet, cook, and eat anything that managed to make it into the boat. At any rate, it was just good to be out.

But that was a long time ago. Still, Harold is actually looking forward to this. It'll be an adventure, man against the wilderness. He's got all the gear — most of it anyway — even though it's pretty ancient. He hopes he can remember how to set up the tent. He should have set it up first before he left, just to air it out. He doesn't worry though, it'll be like riding a bike — if you've done it once, you don't forget.

He's planning to work his way up to a campground on Lake Mahihkan — the Stone's Throw RV Park and Marina. And then navigate around the lake to his cabin, if it's still standing. Hasn't set foot there in three years. He remembers thinking *a stone's throw from where?* There's nothing else around except a few shy cabins peeking from behind the motherly spruce. But there is water, so clear you want to breathe it. You could toss pebbles in the shallows that bordered most of campsites and watch the minnows scatter, a tiny explosion of shimmering darts. It was so peaceful and relaxing. The kids were small then. Life was simple and quiet.

Harold and his grandson now wrestle the canoe from its perch on the Fiesta and carry it to the edge of the water. It's late summer and the flow has ebbed considerably from its spring high. Dragonflies, sun-dancing over the water's surface, always make Harold think of the helicopters he's seen in war movies set in Vietnam. He knew a guy who joined the US Marines so he could go there to fight

Communism. He thought about it himself but the war was over before he got around to it, ending with all those helicopters hovering like dragonflies over hotels in Hanoi. He wonders whatever happed to that guy — he can't even remember his name, Darryl something — if he lived or died, or wanders around blind or with his foot blown off.

They load the canoe. At fifteen feet, it's a bit long for comfortable soloing but it leaves lots of room for his gear, which is stowed in a single, brand-new, large "portage" pack intended to keep things dry from rain, white water, and wind-blown waves. It would even float if it had to. A rifle he hasn't unsheathed from its case in fifteen or twenty years, lays on the canoe floor along with a spare paddle.

His grandson holds the canoe steady while Harold settles aboard. He realizes that he has only a life jacket to soften the bilge against his knees should he need to paddle low in the boat. Too late now. In a moment of panic, he wonders what else he has forgotten.

With a brief shove, Harold is drifting with the current. He turns to see his grandson standing on the shore. The kid raises his hand with a half-hearted wave and yells, "Good luck!"

Harold nods and pretends a smile, then turns to dip his paddle in the water.

He is barely around the first quick bend when a great flood of grief-stricken loneliness washes over him. He has to gasp as though he is drowning. He is grateful no one witnesses the tears flowing down his face.

11

I laugh, of course, despite the pain. As though I would deliberately pour scalding water over my hand.

"Come on," she says, grabbing me by the arm and pulling me from the sink.

"Where?"

"To the hospital. That looks terrible."

I stop, "No, no — it's a scald. They won't do anything for me there that I can't do here. Besides, it's a three hour drive."

"There's a nursing station at the Falls. It's only an hour." She throws a towel under the tap, quickly soaking it. She wraps my hand.

"The Falls" is Pisiw Falls. I was there once fishing as a child with my father, but remember only the swift white water that roared over the deep black rocks. Dave and I used to think the name was very funny, pronounced "piss you."

"Can you imagine coming from Piss You Falls?" I would say.

"Ma-ma-maybe you did," Dave would say.

"Piss you," I would say.

"Piss *you*!" Dave would respond.

"Where are you from?"

"Piss you," Dave would say. And we'd fall on the ground laughing.

I allow myself to be hauled out into the rain, then stop again. "Wait." I rush back into the cabin and grab a bottle.

When we've settled in the Saab and are navigating between black swamp on one side and black spruce on the other, skidding in low spots while trying to avoid boulders that arise unexpectedly out of the Precambrian shield, I lower a window then unwrap my hand and poke it through to let the cold northern rain alleviate the pain.

Dianne says, "Would you close that, please."

I raise the window and drink instead.

I'm already a third way through the bottle and wondering if there is a bar in Pisiw. Or a liquor store. I'll need to stock up.

But when we arrive, it is clear that there is nothing of the sort here.

It is a dry community, adjacent to a dry reserve.

The nursing station in Pisiw Falls is an ATCO Trailer. It is parked alongside other temporary looking, weather-beaten structures with heavy screens over the windows and thick metal doors. *The Northern* in its bold green lettering stands in sharp contrast across the road, immediately adjacent to the "Archie Mackenzie Recreation Complex." I recognize the name of a hockey player from the six-team-NHL days and conclude he must have come from here, but wonder how. Derelict cars and trucks, some with their rusty red bellies facing the clouds, are strewn among the ragged houses set at random depths off the road. The only building with any dignity and grace is the teepee-shaped band office with late model SUVs and trucks parked in front.

"How do you know about this place, Dianne?"

"I was here once, with Dave," she says. "This is where he was from."

◦―◦

She has stopped in front of an ATCO trailer and told me she would wait. I suppose I am pretty much in a state of shock during the treatment given by a very young nurse who wraps my hand while giving me careful instructions on how to care for the injury.

I remember none of them.

I am still stunned by finding Dave's birthplace, not so much by finding it — I wasn't looking — but by Dianne knowing about it.

Aside from performing her nursely tasks, young Florence Nightingale has given me a bottle filled with little white pills.

"I really shouldn't, but you look *responsible*," she says.

"Will these kill me if I take them with alcohol?"

"They won't kill you, no. Unless you take them all at once. You're not going to that, are you?"

"No, no. Not on purpose anyway," I smile.

A brief flicker of alarm appears on her face.

"Of course not," I add before she considers snatching the bottle back from me. "I'm quite responsible."

Dianne would laugh out loud if she heard that.

The nurse has bandaged my hand to look like a small pillow. I protect it as I get back into the Saab. The pain has eased somewhat. I don't know if it's the nurse's white pills or I'm just getting used to it. The burn makes me think of Dave, of course, and all the irony of being in Pisiw Falls.

"Piss You," I say.

"What?" says Dianne, piloting the good ship Saab through the rain.

"Pisiw — Dave and I used to joke about it. How come I didn't know this?"

"There're lots of things . . . "

" . . . 'I don't know about,' Yeah, yeah. So you say."

We pass the Archie Mackenzie Sports Centre.

"Do you suppose he was a relative?"

"Who?"

"Archie Mackenzie. They had the same last name."

"Probably," says Dianne. "Everyone around here is related somehow."

"Did anyone from here come to his funeral?"

"No. They wouldn't have known he died. He tried to find his birth mother once, but she was dead."

"You helped him do this?"

"I came with him, yes. That's how I know this place."

We pass a little girl, perhaps three, who sits splay-legged in a small puddle of water near one of the random houses. She is soaking wet, splashing the water with the flat of her hands — playing. She seems very happy but very alone. She is the only other human being we see in Pisiw Falls, aside from the nurse.

"I'm sorry for tossing that cup."

"You bring that up now?"

"I didn't think it would hit you."

"Who did you think it was going to hit?"

"I thought you'd protect yourself or something."

"Dianne, I was three feet from you."

"You didn't even move."

"Yeah, well . . . " The conversation stalls here. My poor brain is plugged with simultaneous thoughts — *I didn't have* time *to move; I was too drunk to move; I was too surprised to move* — all of which are true. However, mostly I was too enthralled by the teacup floating through the air en route to my face, carried by my sister's rage over the fact that we remember different things when she and Dave flew around the room. And I pulled her out of it — out of the air. " . . . maybe I had it coming," I say.

She opens her mouth to respond, but clamps it shut. Hard. Stares straight ahead.

"What?" I say.

"Nothing," she says.

"You were going to say something. What?"

"Would you turn on the radio? Please?"

"You were going to ask me to turn on the radio?"

"No, but it'll do, won't it? I was going to say you shouldn't mix those pills with your . . . "

"Gin," I help.

"Whatever," she says, "but I know you'd pay absolutely no attention, so I'm just trying to keep my mouth shut."

"Thank you," I say. I turn the radio on to a crackling snatch of Alberta cowboy singing one of those fake hurtin' songs. You can tell it's produced in Nashville, flawless to the point of annoying, Plus, the cowboy's voice is pitch-corrected by computers. Whatever happened to real singing? I turn it off.

"Hey, I liked that song," she says.

I turn it back on, but the reception is so bad that it has disappeared altogether.

"You really don't want to leave it on, do you?"

"No," she says.

"Good. It creeps me out."

She glances at me then asks, "How's your hand?"

"Fine." It is also numb. Whatever the young nurse has given me is working. It almost feels as though the hand is not there. I begin to unwind the gauze wrapped about the burn, flicking the end like a big white ribbon.

"What are you doing?" she says.

"I want to look at it," I say.

"Don't," she says.

"Why not?" I say.

"It'll get infected," she says.

I don't respond to this. I am startled by the colour beneath the wrapping, the thin redness of it.

"Denny, really, don't," she says.

The gauze is on my lap. I lower the window.

"Denny, what are you doing?" she says.

I stick my hand out into the rain.

I lean out the window, the rain stinging my face.

"Davey!" I scream. I hold my hand against the rain as though he can see it. He can't, of course, but I feel a moment of solidarity with his spirit that is part of this black spruce forest nodding in the wind and rain; and in this moment, I believe he actually can see it, and that he nods to acknowledge.

Dianne nearly dumps the Saab into the ditch.

"Sorry," I say.

"I thought you hated that word."

"I do," I say.

"I don't care much for it either," she says.

I slowly rewrap the gauze about my hand, then take another of the young nurse's little white pills. I wash it down with a slug of gin.

Eyes closed, I doze in the car with the nurse's little white helpers, when suddenly my head is slammed forward and we lurch to a halt — eyes wide open.

We are still, tilted to one side — mine — and angled towards a wall of black spruce.

Dianne has a white-knuckled grip on the steering wheel with her arms locked straight. She stares ahead.

"What the fuck happened?" I say.

"Deer." She says. "I swerved to avoid it, and . . . well . . ."

There is no need to explain further.

The Saab is still running, but the gear shift does not respond. We can't move and are hopelessly mired deep in baby-shit clay. We are only a few kilometres from the cell tower at the Stone's Throw. Dianne calls. Someone arrives with a tow truck an hour or so later. Although he hauls us back onto the road with little difficulty, the Saab still refuses to go into gear. Something is broken. We cram into the tow truck's cab. The driver smokes unapologetically. The tire and lube sales pitchmen are cranked up loud.

"I got one of them super antennas," he says. "I can get Texas some nights." The bad, sad country music joins the blue smoke in the cab.

We're on our way to the Ennisville garage.

12

"Fuck," says Harold as he climbs out of the canoe again. He's jammed it up against the shore. Nevertheless, he very nearly dumps it along with himself into what remains of the Mahihkan River, now barely a creek licking its way between the Precambrian rock strewn with windfalls and an astonishing assortment of plastic bags and other debris. As he drags his canoe over the stones, he wonders how all this shit got here.

The dull monotony of solitude, discomfort, and fatigue has him already considering turning back to the bridge from where he began. But he keeps going anyway, dismissing the thought as something a quitter would do, and damn it, he's no quitter.

"Fuck," he says again, alternately tugging and trudging, often backward, until the dry riverbed widens once again into a stream with a foot or two of water and he is able to climb inside the canoe to paddle and pole once more.

The brush billows in thick green tangles from the shore, receding every now and then into small, low meadows of marshy drain or an occasional outcrop of higher rock. A deer and twin fawns, their spots now fading like the foliage around them, startle Harold as they leap in two bounds across the stream and are gone.

Approaching a shallow granite ledge late in the afternoon while trying to shake off the omnipresent insect life around him, Harold suddenly feels self-conscious, as though someone is watching him.

The feeling reminds him of the time when he was twelve and his mother found his stash of nudie mags buried deep in his dresser drawer of socks and underwear — why was she rooting through his underwear? The thought distracts him for a moment, but he remembers the feeling of helpless guilt and a kind of fear. But here, now, although there is not much guilt, there is certainly helplessness and fear, and nothing he can do about it.

As he passes the outcrop, perhaps ten feet away, a wolf turns its head, shifting out of the granite. If it hadn't moved, he would never have seen it standing still now, its yellow eyes clear and forlorn, as though it is caged.

Harold freezes mid-stroke. His canoe drifts briefly before getting caught in the wind and veering towards the rock-strewn shore — towards the wolf. The keel hits the muddy shore. The boat lurches to a halt. They stare at each other for what to Harold seems a very long time. He is disturbed by how unknowable the wolf's eyes are and is unprepared for how terrified and fascinated he can be at the same time. He wonders what the wolf is thinking. Is he sizing him up or merely curious? He does not doubt its capacity for thought. Then the wolf blinks, turns away, and strides into the brush. He swears he can hear it sigh.

As the sky grows darker and darker, Harold looks for a place to drag the canoe ashore so he can pitch his tent, eat, and rest. With increasing anxiety, he paddles, scraping the canoe bottom over stones he can no longer see till he finally seizes upon a small clearing and hopes he can find a patch large and level enough for him to set up for the night.

Barely able to spread his tent — the ground is uneven with a decided pitch towards the water — Harold is going to make do no matter what.

Then it starts to rain.

~∘~∘~

The good thing about the rain is that it keeps the bugs down. The bad thing is everything else. Not only was his soggy tent missing a pole — how could he be missing a single pole! — it has a tear in it the size of a football. Harold has hacked and whittled a piece of willow for the pole, but only watches as water funnels through the tear. He punches a hole in a low spot on the tent's floor and hopes the water will drain out there. Some of it does; the rest is being soaked up by half of his sleeping bag. He crowds up against the high side, bunching the dry half of the bag against his chest away from the wet floor.

His small battery-powered lamp dims. He turns it off. He has spare batteries, somewhere. Everything he owns is inside the black-filled tent, at least half of it now wet. He is hungry but too tired to dig out more than a snack bar that he gobbles in two bites. He falls asleep to the sound of rain beating against the nylon shell between him and the wilderness beyond. He dreams of stones and water and tree branches.

Sometime in the middle of the night, he wakes. The rain has let up. It is quiet now — or, quieter — and mosquitoes have filled the void, entering the tent through the tear in roof. He wants to pull the sleeping bag over his head and ignore them but he has to piss. He finds the little lamp, turns it on and unzips the tent door.

He crawls out of the tent and gets to his feet, disoriented in the dark wet. His hands are so stiff and sore, he cannot find the zipper to his pants. Frustrated, he yanks open his belt and pulls down his pants to let out his cock. After the initial hesitation, the warm relief of letting the piss flow from his body is ecstatic, almost overwhelming. Too soon, however, the mosquitoes have discovered him and he wishes his bladder would empty more quickly.

As he pulls his pants back up, and tucks in his shirt, he suddenly gets that feeling again, that he is being watched. However, without his glasses he can only squint into the dark. Then he thinks he sees some movement by the canoe where he has pulled it up onto the shore, a shadow, now still.

"Gow!!" he yells. He means to say, 'get out', but 'gow' is the sound he makes.

"Hah!" he says, throwing his arms up.

A pair of yellow eyes glint for a second and are gone.

13

We have left the car at the Ennis Garage. The mechanic figures a pin has slipped out of place or is broken. "Hopefully I can jury-rig something to get you south, otherwise you'll be waiting a month for parts. Sweden's a long ways away," he says, the subtext being, "If this was a Chev or Ford, I could have the part tomorrow."

The tow-truck driver, whom we've since found out is Bob's cousin, has given us a ride to the cabin. We are pulling into the lane next to the shed behind the cabin.

"How is your hand?" asks Dianne.

"Still there," I say.

"We should have gone to the cantina to tell Bob what happened."

"He probably knew about it before his cousin did. He'll be just as happy that he doesn't have to pay me."

"Who said you were getting paid?"

"You *volunteered* me?"

"Bob has never paid a musician in his life. Why would he pay you?"

"Well thanks a lot, Dianne. I'll volunteer you to redecorate his house."

I have collected my bottle and its remnants along with the pills, awkward with only one hand, and with them tucked against my chest, I struggle to get into the cabin. Dianne has detoured to the outhouse which was upgraded twenty years ago to include a flush toilet. Inside, I set my drugs on the table.

The fire in the stove has just about died. I poke at the remaining embers. I've been in charge of the fire since we've arrived, and suddenly, this is no longer possible — well, possible, but no longer easy. Dianne enters, slamming the door behind her.

"This weather is the shits," she says.

"It's not snowing," I say.

"Yeah well, we still need a fire. Let me," says Dianne taking the poker from me. "You might as well take it easy."

There is a weariness in her voice, mixed, I am sure, with a little disgust.

Doing what I can to help, I reach for an old newspaper from a stack beside the woodbin. And there, now uncovered, sitting atop the stack, is a handwritten page. This is what it says:

"Amigo. No hay mas importante que comiendo. There is nothing more important than eating. What I cannot get in this place is cilantro. Everything else I can find — jitomate, cebolla, pimiento, limon y tambien las muchachas. You know what I'm talking about. I am dying for salsa picante. Do what you can. I will make it worth your while. Cesar."

I hand it to Dianne. She goes to throw it in the stove now afire with kindling.

"Whoa! Dianne, not in the fire. I think you should read it first."

She looks at it. Takes it in. "'*Las muchachas?*' That's not part of the recipe."

"Young girls," I say. And look at the name."

She gets it immediately. "Oh, your Spanish AA book. Well, isn't that a coincidence." She says this with more than a suggestion of sarcasm.

"Yes." A remarkable coincidence. It gives me the creeps. The ooga-booga factor is rising. I have risen to my feet and picked up the book, the *Reflexiones Diarias*, from where I left it beside my guitar case. I hand it to her.

"What?" she says.

"Cremate it too," I say.

She looks at me for an instant then tosses the book into the flames.

There is something purging in the act, expiation, an acknowledgment of something almost spiritual. There are degrees of evil masked in good — the better the mask, the greater the evil. If I ever come out of this, it will not be through AA. And whoever Cesar Guzman might be or might have been — drug cartel? — his route through AA in prison with my brother pimping food and girls for him while he assured Dave it would be worth his while, is somehow really creepy and repulsive, maggots feeding on maggots. The urge to retch is physical. I go out into the rain and heave up everything inside me — of which there is not a whole lot.

I stand on the back porch for a long time, letting the rain wash the bile off my face, getting wet and wondering why I'm reacting like this. I am wondering if I am grieving, if this is what grief is all about.

⌒⌒

The pill and gin combination — not to mention the news regarding Dave's birthplace and Cesar Guzman's note — has put me in a reflective mood. Introspective. Philosophical. Paranoid. Hallucinogenic. A variant on normal, just a bit more intense.

Dianne has scrambled some eggs and fried some bacon because you can eat breakfast anytime at the lake even if it's the dimming of the day. I can't recall the last time I had bacon and eggs. It may have been the last time I was here, fifteen or twenty years ago when Dad was still alive. Dad was a big bacon-and-eggs man. I am not. I am a toast-and-coffee man, but I eat it all anyway to be a good sport. I don't think Dianne is a big bacon-and-eggs eater either, judging by the way she picks and prods at her plate.

However, she finishes — or really, just stops eating — and I take the plates to the sink, offering to wash them. I know that Dianne will decline my offer, and she does. I am not sure why I go through the motions of this little charade, it is so bogusly transparent. But I do.

I unwrap my hand again and think of mummies. But my hand is not mummified, it is lobster-ied. Lobster red.

I pull Mr. Martin from his case and form a few tentative chords — D, A, but G hurts. The stretch, small as it is, is simply too painful. I wonder how many tunes I know in D and A. E also works. I think I could do a short blues set. The B7 is very uncomfortable. I wonder if I can get used to it. I wonder if Dave got used to it. Is it just something you learn to live with and just carry on?

I get an idea that maybe if I open tune the guitar, I'll be able to use a bottleneck. I pull apart a salts, haker and dump the salt on the table.

"Denny!" says Dianne.

"For my art," I say. I'm suddenly excited about the possibilities; I haven't played in public for years, even if it is at Bob's cantina — for nothing. I work up a few bars of *Dust My Broom*. It's not Elmore James, but it's something.

"That doesn't sound *too* bad," says Dianne. "Does this mean you will play at Bob's?"

"Maybe. In a couple of days. If it doesn't hurt too bad."

I rewrap my hand and return Mr. Martin to his velvet-lined coffin. No point in overdoing it.

I can feel the darkness closing in. The rain has let up, but the wind lashes.

14

The morning is no better than the previous night, lighter, maybe, but noticeably cooler, and windy. The rain could start any minute.

Harold wants to start a fire but there is not a stick of dry wood anywhere. There is not a dry anything anywhere. He thinks briefly of setting his tent aflame for all the good the damn thing did. He knows it would simply flare up for a moment then congeal into a stinking lump. He would give his right eye for a cup of coffee, never mind it doesn't work too well; it's why he has the glasses.

After his encounter with the yellow-eyed shadow, he had returned to his tent and stuffed his jacket into the hole hoping it would stop the mosquitoes from feeding off him and muffle their incessant whining. Proof that he slept at all are the red welts their bites left on his wrist and forehead. Still tired and hungry, he tips the canoe on its side to empty most of the water and realizes he left his gun lying in the bilge. Its canvas case is soaked. Then he collects the rest of his gear, rolls everything into a wet ball, tosses it into the canoe, and pushes back into the river. His hands are sore from the previous day and he wishes he had gloves.

Gloves, what a stupid oversight, like the missing tent pole; it reminds him that he really has no business doing this. That it is a pathetic gesture of self-pity. What if he gets hurt? Who would he notify? *How* would he notify? But as much to the point, who would care? Maybe his grandson. Maybe.

His grandson helped him plot the course on his GPS so he does know where he is — he's the little blue dot in the middle of the screen. If he shrinks the map enough, he can tell what province he's in. Up here it looks like there's as much water as land. He wonders why he keeps scraping bottom. He's got to remember not to leave the thing on too long or the battery will die, and maybe him along with it, although he glumly figures that he'll much more likely die of starvation or exposure even with the help of his GPS. He bought it for his truck to help him navigate through cities. It was a godsend, a real miracle of technology. He was not one of those guys who lived on his CB radio. He had one, but rarely turned it on now. What is he thinking, "now"? There is no "now". Now he's in a canoe wishing he could take a piss and knowing he'll have to stop soon to do just that. There's no leaning over the gunwale and dropping your drawers in a canoe, not if you wanted to stay dry, anyway, even though dry is relative in Harold's case.

As the hours pass, the river widens somewhat and the speed of the current eases. He paddles now to correct his angles and keep close to shore. He has scooped a few handfuls of water to slack his thirst. He hasn't taken his piss pills yet and doesn't like to miss them. "Hypertension, the silent killer," the brochure read. It might get him at any time. He could just croak right here and no one would ever know. They'd find the canoe overturned and empty somewhere downstream. His body would sink, then rise a few weeks later, bloated, minus his eyeballs that fish or birds would have snacked on.

He really has to eat. These thoughts are doing him no good.

As he rounds another bend in the river, he sees a flash of red on the bank. It's a canoe, or the remnants of one, overturned in the grass. It is the same colour as his but with its ribs exposed and rotting away from the frame like the carcass of a dead thing. Then, twenty or thirty yards back into the woods, a cabin, black with age and barely visible through the bush.

Harold's heart now beats with the excitement of the vision — that and the exertion of pulling his boat onto the shore. He stands in his soggy clothes and relieves himself onto a stone lying amid sedge. He is mesmerized by the splashing flecks. He should remember his damn piss pills, not that they would ease the situation.

After shaking off the last reluctant drops and tucking himself back in, he trudges through the wet fen, past three sun-bleached poles poking skyward at odd angles. There were four, but he steps over one that has fallen to the ground. He surmises that when they all stood erect, they composed a frame for drying skins or fish. He has seen pictures of this somewhere — a book? He doesn't read many books. Must have been on TV. Then he stumbles to catch his balance. One foot has caught in a scrap of half-rotted netting. He reaches down to remove it. *Volleyball?* he thinks. *No,* he chides himself, *they* fish *with nets.* Volleyball, he decides, is the kind of conclusion Reta would have come to. He wonders why he ends up

140

thinking of her at the oddest times. "Volleyball," he says aloud.

When he reaches the derelict cabin, he peers past the battered door that hangs by a single hinge. Harold is careful to pull it straight thinking that this might well be a place where he can dry out and eat.

Inside are the remains of a small bedframe, a stump that might have been used as a chair and a box that likely served as a table. There is no window. Two empty shelves hang from the rough log wall. Still more or less intact, a small barrel sits on a mound of rocks with a two-foot section of rusted stove pipe standing on it, capped by an elbow poking through the wall. It's like air to a drowning man, blue in a sky of grey.

In no time, he has ripped apart the bedframe and watches it crackle cheerful red flames inside the barrel stove. Although he can see dreary grey light split between the logs once chinked with clay, the roll roofing is remarkably tight and the dirt floor is powdery dry. He will lay out his tent and attempt a patch as soon as he is done eating. The water has almost come to a boil in the small pot he has included with his provisions, and he has torn open an envelope of dried food, "hearty beef stew", for which his mouth is watering. When he thinks the water is hot enough, he dumps the package into the pot, stirring the contents with a spoon. He can't remember the last time he was so hungry.

He has made several trips back and forth to the canoe, hauling pretty well everything in it back to the cabin. It weighs twice as much as it did when he set sail yesterday — only one full day and it feels like a lifetime.

Harold is not a religious man but he remembers when he was very young saying grace before his mother let him eat, often hot porridge for breakfast and cold porridge for lunch, then pork and beans for supper, which he hated. But being hungry and saying grace somehow made the food taste better. He realizes they must have been very poor. But no one complained. That was just life. It's the way things were. And now he finds himself thanking God for providing the hearty beef stew. Nonsense, he knows. He should really be thanking his grandson for making him take the plastic pouches of freeze-dried trail food, something he never knew existed. His plan had been to live off the land — fish and shoot his own game — never mind this river has long since been fished out, he hasn't hunted in twenty odd years, and he's not even certain that the gun works. He makes a mental note to check it out.

Although the rain has stopped, a bleak drizzle has settled in and he needs more fuel for the stove. He ventures out behind the cabin where it seems less sodden under the aspen canopy and finds a stack of wood leaning up against the back wall. He can't believe his luck. Much of it is rotted, but there are a few good pieces, more or less dry, that he can stoke the stove with. Even though it's early in the afternoon, he's decided to spend the night here where he'll be warm and dry. He is almost giddy with relief.

Carrying several armloads inside, it occurs to him that someone has cut this wood and very likely intended to use it. He wonders what happen to them. Did they die? Are their bones lying in the woods somewhere? Or did they just move back to wherever they came from? How long has this place been abandoned? Or has it been abandoned? Maybe it's only in use part-time, seasonally.

He explores a little more carefully the inside of the cabin and notices a pile of pine-cone shells, or maybe it's spruce or fir, he's not sure, anyway, the remnants of a squirrel's stash. Now he knows he's not the only interloper that has spent time in this shelter. On the wall near the stove, several stout pegs protrude where pots or clothes or snowshoes might have been impaled, and beneath one of them, a set of initials, "RM".

RM. Rural Municipality, he thinks. He wonders which one. Then *Richard Mackenzie,* RM, his wife's favourite soap opera doctor. His initials were always emblazoned on his white coat pocket. No doc he ever knew had their initials on their pocket. But RM did. A Camry man for sure. That's when it all started going to rat shit, he thinks, when they got the second TV. He would be watching hockey or the news or whatever, and she would be watching Richard Mackenzie.

Fuck, why is he thinking about her again? The RM who carved his initials into the wall is not a soap opera star — maybe a Robert or a Ralph. Ralph, a common enough name around these parts, and he knows several of them. There are legions of Mackenzie's, guys whose great-grandmothers never saw a white man till they paddled ashore with their Hudson's Bay blankets, guys whose great-grandfathers never tasted a drop of booze, and now, in some annual right of retribution, spend the winter months on the trap line to halt their addictions, to purify and remind themselves of who they are. Some of the Ralphs live clean and decent and sober lives after their winters of abstinence. Harold hopes that the Ralph of this camp is one.

Now, seated on the stump and chewing on his "hearty beef stew," Harold decides that while it is filling the hole in his gut, it is unlike any beef stew he has ever eaten before. He is slightly disappointed but nevertheless acknowledges it is doing the job, although it could have a flavour more akin to actual food. It is slightly bitter and utterly bland. It reminds him of the tofu Reta once tried to get him to eat. He wasn't having any of it. He looks again at the package, adjusting his glasses and reads more carefully. "Hearty Beef Stew", then, in smaller, less conspicuous lettering, the words, "soy food product with artificial flavouring."

He glumly swallows and continues eating, pondering the identity of RM who would certainly not be eating soy food product. Harold imagines him, dark, leather-faced, and wiry-lean holed up in his cabin on a cold winter's night with nothing but his coal oil lamp and the wind whipping at the door — back when it had both hinges — with a good fire in his stove and maybe a pot of . . . what? . . . maybe beaver, did trappers eat beaver? He doesn't know. Rabbit, then. Or maybe a chunk of moose he shot with this thirty-ought-six, the same kind of gun that he himself carries — which reminds him, that now would be a good time to check it out, maybe clean it and see if it still works. Of course it would still work. Why wouldn't it?

The gun has been lying in the bottom of the canoe in its ancient and soaked canvas case since yesterday afternoon when he put the boat into the water. With it now removed, he can turn the canoe upside down to prevent more water from sloshing about its bilge.

Back in the cabin, he has hung the case on one of the pegs and attempts to dry the stock and barrel with the sleeve of his shirt — now relatively dry. He admires the gun, likes its heft and the feel of it in his hands. He opens the bolt, and out pops a brass cartridge. Except it is not a cartridge; it is a live, taper-tipped bullet. *Holy shit*! he thinks, *I could have blown my leg off.* He knows this is unusual, that he is normally very careful about emptying the chamber of his rifle. He tries to remember the last time he cleaned it. Can't. It's been a long time. He pulls the bolt back half way, putting his finger behind the trigger and pushing it forward. It is stiff with disuse but with some effort he pulls the bolt out. He then sights through the barrel, expecting to see light out the other end. There is none. Wondering what he can use to prod down the bore, he considers using one of his tent poles. *Too fat*, he thinks. What would Ralph use in a situation like this? Maybe a twig, a willow branch.

Whatever is lodged in the barrel won't budge. It is only about six inches in and jammed there. Harold feels a brief chill. "I'll kill you," he remembers Reta warning him, "one way or another." He thought it was just talk, an idle threat, a stupid game they played, like when he locked her in the basement. That was where he kept the gun. He can see her now putting the bullet into the chamber and jamming the bore with whatever it is. He hadn't left her down there for long — maybe an hour. He remembers how strangely quiet she was when he let her back up. Quiet and smug. He could have pulled that trigger and he would be lying there dead or bleeding to death, and no one would ever have known.

She was really going to kill me. It's a sobering thought. He's not sure what to make of it, whether he should be pissed off or merely amazed that her hatred was actually that intense. That somewhere down the line, she expected him to come into great harm.

This is not the way he ever imagined facing death. He is surprised by how calm he feels — that and a little surprised that someone he knew would deliberately set out to kill someone else. He thinks of it in the third person, that the someone is not himself, and the someone he knew was not the mother of his children, the grandmother to his grandson. It was so purposeful, requiring two separate acts, loading the chamber and jamming the bore.

It was not like his pissing in a bottle at all, even though it had a far worse effect — that had been completely and totally unintentional. But it did cause somebody to die. Nevertheless, she is wherever the hell she is, and he is here, in a rotting cabin in the rain somewhere in the middle of nowhere. And he is here because he killed someone.

Harold sits on the floor. The strength has left his legs, and he sits because he cannot stand. He would collapse if he tried. Perhaps he has collapsed. This is what collapsing is like, he tells himself. This is what killing a person feels like, even if you didn't mean it.

It has never occurred to him before. All this while he has been concerned only about himself. And he is alive. The biker is dead. And Harold has killed him.

He doesn't even know his name. He cannot recall if his name was mentioned in court. He wonders now who he is, who he might have been, why there was no family weeping in the courtroom. He would have remembered that, like he remembers his high-school-age lawyer, and the judge who put him in mind of his wife. He could not forget those things. It only occurs to him now. The whole event is a series of blurry disconnected images, like bits of a movie with a crackling, broken soundtrack. He supposes the name must have been stated by one of the cops or someone during the endless drone of testimony. The fact that he can't remember it, or little else really, reinforces his notion that he has felt nothing through this, no remorse or concern for anyone other than himself. It has left him with a loathing for everything and everyone; they can all just fuck off — save for his grandson and maybe RM, whoever he is, and possibly the dead biker, whoever he *was*. He even loathes himself; *I am such a stupid fuck.*

The conclusion, though, puts him at peace — there is nothing he can do about it now. He is doomed and alone, but okay with it. He will continue his journey through the woods in his canoe, eventually arrive at the Stone's Throw, and maybe get a job there for a few months, till he can drive again. Maybe wash dishes in Bob's restaurant, or chop wood for him, the wood that he sells at an exorbitant rate to the campers swatting mosquitoes in his campground, though the campers would be thinning out now. Something like that. No, he won't be living off the land now, not without a gun. And what would he shoot anyway? Deer? Fawns? Wolves? *Try cooking a wolf*, he tells himself. *Ha*!

The light of the day is shifting now to darkness. There is no sun, and if he did not have his GPS, he would not know which way was north or south. Not that it matters, he is a speck in the middle of the universe, patching the hole in his tent. There is just enough room to pitch it inside the cabin and he does so to make the mending task easier. He has also decided that he will sleep in it to protect himself from the swarming mosquitoes who seem to have found the warmth of the cabin as appealing as he has.

When he lays himself on top of his almost-dry sleeping bag, having stripped and hung his clothes on the wall pegs and having taken his piss pill and removed his glasses, he savours the warmth and the sound of the falling rain. He is dry and bug free. He is as happy as he has been in a long time. Happy may not be the right word — content. At peace with himself. He doesn't know why, but he is not going to argue. He accepts it, welcomes it, just as he accepts and welcomes the sleep that settles into him.

In the middle of the night, he wakens. He has to piss. It takes him a moment to remember where he is. He disentangles himself from the tent, opens the door to the cabin, and relieves himself into the rain. He stuffs two more pieces of firewood in the barrel stove before returning to his tent. It is cooler now. He gets inside the sleeping bag. Sleep comes quickly again.

When he rises soon after daylight, he is stiff and sore — but dry. He steps out the cabin door to relieve himself again but lying there, directly in front of the door, is the foreleg of deer. Perhaps of a fawn. It is tiny and delicate, still covered in fur. It is cut off neatly at the knuckle of what would be the elbow, whatever that joint is called on deer. He kicks it away from the door.

In twenty minutes, he has loaded the canoe and pushed off, but not before removing the bolt to his thirty-ought six and tossing both it and the gun into the river.

15

We've retired to what once passed as a veranda. It had been tacked onto the south side of the cabin to provide shade on those rare summer days when the sun actually shone. It is wrapped in a screen cocoon, mostly torn and patched over with various thicknesses of plastic, much of which has yellowed or is utterly opaque with time.

Dianne has taken a break from her knitting, but I'll be able to continue drinking till I fall over or run out — whichever comes first. She has wrapped herself in her sleeping bag, huddled herself into an ancient easy chair that I hope isn't too overrun with mice. I don't say anything, but one scampers across the sagging floor behind her.

We are blithering about this and that, ignoring the contents of the day and the reason we are here. But we pretend we are philosophizing — at least I do. The year I went to university, I took a philosophy class, Philosophy 120. It was an introductory course where we were supposed to explore the fundamental problems about reality — not *real* reality, but the *idea* of reality. I never got to first base because I just loved the *idea* of philosophy; it meant you were smart or had some sort of inclination towards *wisdom* and it gave you a kind of credibility, a substance, a *weight*. I thought that thinking about thinking would be a snap — I did it all the time. Turned out there was more to it than that. We were expected to understand the limits of human knowledge and the nature of the mind, like if we have free will and so forth. We had to write essays that were supposed to develop our arguing and researching skills, make us better writers, use the tools of the philosophers' trade. It's a trade like anything else, and I couldn't even learn how to operate the tools, much less apply them — or learn and remember who applied *what* tools *when* — which was really what the class was about. Ontology, epistemology. I flunked so badly, it wasn't even a joke.

But I still loved the class. I loved being among people who actually understood, or seemed to understand what they were talking about. Maybe they didn't, but they were great fakers if they didn't because they could riff on ideas like musicians riff on a four-beat bar. It gave me a kind of comfortable feeling, like a really great jam — even though I'm just following the chords and not really contributing, I'm in the middle, feeling the rhythm, and I'm a part of it.

So that's what I'm feeling tonight with Dianne. But I am contributing. I'm riffing. It's music. It doesn't mean anything, it's just music — noise, measured tones with rhythm and space. Blither. I'm *in* it.

Dianne, though, maybe not so much.

"So if you have fun dying, it's okay," she says again.

"Absolutely! You might not be able to choose your death — but you can certainly choose your fun," I say proudly.

"You've never made a choice in your life," says Dianne. "That's why you're about . . . " she holds her thumb and index finger an inch apart, "that deep."

"I make choices every day — even if . . . " I hold my thumb and index finger an inch apart, "I'm only that deep."

"All your choices are about avoiding making choices."

"Those are choices."

"No they aren't. That's just going with the flow. You're not making any decisions, because to make decisions you have to have some depth — and you don't have any depth, Denny. You trivialize everything."

"We just don't value the same things, Dianne. I don't trivialize things that I value."

"Name one. Name one thing you value, besides what you're holding in your hands."

She's referring to my teacup, of course, cradled amid the gauze on one hand and raven's claws on the other.

"I value my hands too, you know. That's two things, especially the scalded one. If you want to break it down further, I value all ten fingers too. That's twelve things."

"See! You're trivializing! Even the things you value! And the reason you trivialize everything is because you don't have any courage to face things as they are. So you make them less. That's why you can't get any women to stay with you . . . "

"I make them less? Well, they're not much to begin with. I mean, they're not making the best choices either — witness their choice of me."

"See! That's why you can't make a living as a musician. You make *yourself* less. You just swim around. You're like some sort of fish with no fins, and you float along on top this foggy sea, wondering, 'Where the hell am I?'"

Dianne is on a roll. Poetry, no less. I hate to stop her. "I know exactly where I am. And please spare me the metaphor."

"Yeah, right! And where is that?"

"Well, actually, I'm not there yet." It's difficult to explain to someone who has never been there, wherever *there* is — *the Zone*. I suppose it may well be a foggy sea, but it feels like a kind of colour, an amber — a deep amber, almost a sepia, the colour of fading sunsets and old westerns. But it's more than that. There's a time element to it as well. Time slows, becomes clearer, cleaner. It does float. Floating sepia. Sea-pee-yeah. See Pisiw. "However, I'm on my way." I offer a brief toast, raising my chipped teacup. "Piss you," I say.

Dianne shakes her head. "Kirsten is just like you. And you are just like Dad."

This stops me. I didn't expect to arrive here, being compared to Kirsten and Dad. This is not company I cherish.

"I guess it runs in the family."

"I guess it does," she agrees.

"You just never know, do you, how people are going to turn out."

"Unless it runs in the family," she corrects.

"Red hair runs in the family, but it seems to have skipped me."

"All hair skipped you, Denny."

I do not quibble with the fact that I am bald. In our baby pictures, we pose — happy, smiling, and *bald*. We can't help it; we're like all babies even though some go missing or are murdered by their parents. There is no telling from the photographs who will live with hair and who will not, or who will live in terror and who in peace. We were all happy smiling babies. What happens between then and now? Why so many sad, frowning adults? Why so many pinched faces? How do we end up so dead in the bottom of an urn?

"Fuck," I say.

"What?" says Dianne.

"I didn't plan on being bald. I didn't decide it."

"We're not talking about your being bald, Denny."

"I know. We're talking about how people wind up where they are, and you think we choose to be there, even if we don't choose it, and I think shit happens."

"I think we choose our own shit — or, don't choose it, as in your case."

"Of all the non-choices I never made, I never made one that I regretted — none."

"None?"

"None."

"If I could figure out what you just said . . . "

"Okay, one — I never said goodbye to Dad."

"Oh, give me a break."

"I didn't. I regret it."

I had the chance too, but I never did it. Dianne is right, I didn't have the guts. I felt so sorry for the sonofabitch. He was not a nice man. He was not nice to anybody, not even Dianne — forget me and Dave. Push me out in the cold when it's forty below. There are reasons for things. "Go get a job; help out." I was twelve. So I get that paper route. It's so cold, birds would fall out of the sky. They'd lie there on the steps, their little feet sticking up in the air. This is to teach me responsibility, Dad said — frozen birds with their feet in the air. And then I got that route in the hospital, St. Stephen's Hospital *of Hope*. People called it, "The Hope," or, "The Hopeless," depending on whether you went there to live or to die. It didn't bother me one way or the other; I was warm. I loved that route.

Dave, a year older, a year bigger, gets a job pumping gas at Les'. He didn't have to talk much — "Fif-ill?" "Oil?" He liked it. It was his introduction to grease and wrenches. Every car on the south side went to Les' for servicing. Nobody could figure out why it was called what it was called because it was owned by a family of Torchinskis — all men — except for Mrs. Torchinski whose name was Eleanor. It was a mystery till Dave found out there had been a daughter, Leslie, who was hit by a car and died when she was a little girl. So they named the garage after her. Sad but true.

Back at the hospital, St. Stephen's, there was this little canteen, in the basement where I used to pick up my papers to sell — *The Blind Canteen*. It was run by this blind guy, Tony, so that's why it's called the Blind Canteen. Tony was amazing. He was totally blind, but it didn't bother Tony because he could see with his hands. He knew where everything was, the chocolate bars, cigarettes, combs, the Kleenex, and he was very comfortable with this. Elegant. Graceful. You'd ask him what time it was, and tell you, "Ten minutes past four!" I couldn't figure out how he did this day after day. Eventually, I asked him. He said, "Give me your hand," and he put my fingers on the watch face where a small latch clicked open the glass and I could feel the hands and the little bumps beside the numbers. He performed this task for me, one step at a time, but he'd normally done it so quickly, it looked like he'd just passed his hand over his watch. "Ten minutes past four!" Magic.

But on his days off, this other guy would come in and take his place. I would know that he was in the Canteen before I ever entered it for his creepy, weird billy goat laugh. He wore thin, wire-rimmed glasses with lenses so thick they made his eyes look like onions with little black bugs in the middle. However, he could see a little bit — shades, shadows, whatever — but he was as uncomfortable with the little bit that he could see as Tony was comfortable being totally blind.

My papers would be sitting on this little counter, where you could sit on a stool and have a coke, but I never saw anyone ever sit there, except once, and that was Onion Eyes himself. He had one of my newspapers unfolded in front of him and he was pretending to be reading it. The reason I know he was pretending to read the paper is because it was upside down. Upside down in front of him, and he looked up at me and smiled as if to say, "See, I'm reading the paper." I couldn't tell him it was upside down because there wasn't any point to it. I just remember feeling so sorry for this stupid adult who is pretending to read and he's not fooling anyone, not even me and I'm only twelve years old.

I've done my route. Outside, in the Hope parking lot, I see a car just like ours — a blue 1956 Ford two-door. It is ours! Dad is on his knees changing a rear tire. I think for a minute that he's actually come to pick me up, something he's never done before. Then I notice the car next to ours is slightly off-kilter too, and I realize that my dad is removing the tire on the car next to ours — he's switching them.

My dad is a thief.

I turn around. I walk to the bus stop like I always do. I go home. I don't say anything to anybody. What do you say? At supper he tells Mom that he got some new tires — cheap because they don't match, and not exactly new, but newish, better than what we had.

My dad is a thief and a liar. And I just remember feeling so fucking mad at this stupid adult who's pretending to be honest, and he's fooling everyone, except me, and I'm only twelve years old.

Dianne is wrong. I am not like Dad. I am not a thief or a liar. And although I'm a drunk, I read the newspaper upside right. I tell time by raising my eyes across the sky. I make music. Sometimes.

I have arrived in the Zone. I don't know how long I've been silent, or even *if* I've been silent — I may have been talking the whole while — but Dianne suddenly screams and scrambles to her feet, crouching on the chair. She does this in a single motion. She has startled me to the extent I've splashed gin all over my bandaged hand. It actually offers some relief, although I can now imagine myself sucking it.

"What?" I'm not sure why I ask because I know my little furry friend has returned from wherever he was. Maybe looking for a lost relative.

"A mouse," she says, looking insofar as she is able without tipping off the chair. "Where did it go?"

"Dianne, the place is full of mice. There are so many mice, they are committing suicide — throwing themselves down our well."

"Ha-ha," she says. This is no laughing matter.

"Maybe they're being executed, murdered. Maybe they're committing mouse-icide."

"That is not even remotely funny," she says, climbing back down off the chair. "And I don't believe a word you said about Dad."

16

A pair of ravens sits high on the bank, waiting in black spruce or Jack pine after every bend in the river. Harold can't tell if they are the same two leading him along, or a long line of sentinels guiding his route. Whichever they are, he decides he likes them, along with the various sounds they make that range from a croaky bray to an intimate, grandmotherly clucking — like pebbles dropped into a wooden bucket half full of water.

He's either getting used to it or starting to like it, he can't tell which, but the quiet solitude has energized him despite the cool, wet, blowy weather.

He knows he is getting close to civilization because he can actually smell it — gasoline, or is it oil? It surprises him that after only three days in the wilderness he can detect this. He wonders if he is imagining it, then he sees a rainbow amid the bulrushes next to shore — a small oil slick.

This upsets him; he somehow expects more of people but then realizes, why should he? He's the one farting diesel fumes into the atmosphere all his working life. How can he talk or be surprised? Oil. Here. Making pretty rainbows on the water. Fuck.

Then he hears something, or rather notices that the omnipresent still-and-quiet has been altered, and not by the ravens who still seem to be following him, but something else, something bigger. He's heard it before but he can't put his finger on it. And it is growing louder.

Then he sees it.

White water tumbling over rocks.

Right in front of him.

He knew he'd heard the sound before, at Niagara Falls where he and Reta honeymooned, when they could afford it, five years after their marriage.

This is it, he thinks. *I'm going to die.*

His instinct is to just grip the canoe gunnel and hang on. But this, he knows, is not the manly thing to do. Scanning the gorge, he sees a swift-moving, dark channel devoid of rocks. If he can manage to reach it before the white water reaches him, he should be okay. With all his strength, he draws his right side, hoping to propel the canoe and keep it from going broadside to the current. But the canoe is sluggish with its length and weight; he does not have the strength to power across the flow.

Gritting his teeth, he knows now he must shoot these rapids like an outdoorsman, like he knows what he's doing. Never mind he doesn't have a clue. The worst of the white evil pounding and roiling stretches before him for perhaps a hundred yards or so, but it might as well be endless for all the hope he has of making it through dry. In fact, dry would be a miracle; he'd settle for wet and alive. He wonders when his life will begin flashing before him. He tries to recall his first memories — was it in grade one that he melted his crayons, pressing them against the classroom radiator, watching the colours drip onto the floor? Yes, and Melanie Forschuk squealed on him. She squealed on everybody. He can still see her tiny white tattle-tale hand pumping in the air, "Miss! Miss! Harold is melting crayons . . . "

Holy shit! he thinks. *This is how it happens.* His life *is* flashing before him — well, not exactly *flashing*. It's a slow motion replay for which he has no time as he digs his paddle to avoid a huge boulder the size of a Volkswagen, knowing that even if he manages to evade the VW, he will be torn apart by the shark-toothed rock below it.

Which is exactly what happens.

The canoe jars to a sudden halt. In that split second where time expands to watch itself unfold, he flies through the air, conscious of being surprised the collision wasn't a more dramatic crunch, not the loud dull *drum-thud*. Time stops completely as he is pitched onto his back and tumbled upside down, shocked by the heavy cold and darkness. He doesn't know which way is up.

This is when Harold sees God. He is an old man with a white beard, just as he suspected. Standing beside Him is Harold's smiling mother and younger sister who died years before. He briefly wonders where his dad is. He is surprised by his inner serenity; he is ready to relax, to give in to the experience — to die — but Reta stands next to his sister, and he suddenly knows this isn't a glimpse of heaven.

He is jolted with a wicked energy.

Time returns.

The canoe and its contents ride the waves over and beyond him.

Between gulps of air and frantic flailing, he scrambles and washes towards the shore. *I'm not dead yet,* he thinks before he loses consciousness, his head striking a rock.

When Harold comes to, he is immediately aware of two things: a huffing breath (not his) and a pain in his jaw. It is not exactly like a toothache, but similar. More slowly, he becomes aware of the rest of his body. It is immensely heavy and cold. It does not feel at all right.

He tries to focus on the huffing coming from directly behind him. He realizes he is being pulled from the water onto the shore and that whoever is doing the huffing has hold of the back of his life jacket collar and is tugging him an inch at a time. He tries to turn to see who it is, twisting, but his legs and arms are filled with icy lead. He can't. Not yet. He flexes his fingers instead. It's a start. There is a smell though, familiar but misplaced. He is satisfied he's not dead. Yet.

He thinks impossible thoughts, like wondering if his piss pills are okay, and if the deer leg in front of RM's cabin was for real, like the brief and almost imperceptible thump he heard or felt when the bus passed him those few weeks back, tossing a biker under his wheels.

He can now feel the backs of his legs bumping over the rocks in the shallows. His shoulders are above water. The tugging stops.

Gathering all his strength, Harold tries to turn onto his side and stretch to see behind him, to see who has been pulling him from the water, but is distracted by something nudging his leg.

It's a paddle. He pulls it up beside him and uses it to help him sit up. He wonders how this is possible. *How could the paddle arrive here after me?* Then he notices a large eddy nearby with his backpack along with other debris swirling in it. It transfixes him. Every now and then, a small branch or leaf will seem to escape its orbit only to be dragged back in. He can't understand how the paddle escaped the vortex.

He rubs his eyes and realizes his glasses are gone. He scans the bank behind him, squinting. Something rustles in the tangle of brush. His sense of being watched returns. He becomes conscious of a raven's call, the hoarse "haw-haw" and catches a glimpse of a pair — the pair? — flying off in tandem beyond the next bend in the river. They are out of focus.

He pats his soggy jacket pocket, trying to feel his packet of waterproof matches. They are not there. He remembers they are in his backpack. He pats his wallet pocket. For what it's worth, the little money he has is also still intact. *All the good it does,* he thinks.

The roar that was ahead of him earlier is now behind him, and much less noisy. Although he aches everywhere, he has risen to his feet and probes for his backpack with his paddle. He leans out over the water, hanging onto a willow branch with one hand, and pokes at the pack with the other. He disturbs it, sets it free. But rather than drifting ashore nearby, it bobs jauntily further downstream.

"Fuck," says Harold as he staggers along the shoreline using the paddle half for support and half to propel him on. However, the pack disappears from sight, around the same bend the ravens took.

When he finally reaches the bend, he sees it opens into a small lake, maybe half a kilometre wide and twice as long. His backpack has settled amid some lily pads close to shore. Retrieving it, he begins to look for a clearing, a way into the woods where he might find some dry wood. He needs to build a fire to dry out, to thaw. He knows hypothermia is a real danger now, and just because he didn't drown doesn't mean he can't find other ways to die.

He hears a boat motor approach from the other end of the lake. He makes himself as big as possible and waves the paddle. "Hey! Hey!" he calls.

The people in the boat don't seem to recognize the trouble Harold is in. They have stopped several hundred metres out and are occupied with some task that Harold cannot make out. Finally, they throttle their motor and turn towards him.

Harold can make out two bodies, one of them very large and round, the other as tall but thin. The larger one speaks.

"Did you lose your canoe?" he asks.

"Yes," says Harold, nodding.

"It tried to go on without you," says the thin man. He grins at his joke, showing gaps where his teeth should be.

Behind their beat-up Lund, a red canoe bumps up against the stern. "Is this it?" asks the round man as he hauls it around his boat.

"Yes, it's mine," answers Harold. Or at least that's what he tries to say. He's not sure what sounds came out of his mouth. He is now aware that it is swollen — probably his whole face is swollen.

"You don't look too good," says the thin man.

Although Harold cannot see them clearly, he can tell by their accents and how they phrase things that their first language is Cree, or maybe Dene — he can't tell the difference. Anyway, they are northerners, trappers or fishermen, as familiar with the woods and water as he is the cab of a truck.

"We better get you dried off," says the round man. With Harold protesting weakly, they climb from their boat, sit Harold on a stone, and throw a sleeping bag over his shoulders while they build a fire.

In less than two hours, Harold is feeling nine-tenths dry and holding a hot cup of tea. He offers to "pay for their trouble," but the thin man just shakes his head and smiles, "No, no. Maybe you can help us out sometime."

As they push off, the keel of the Lund scraping over the stones, Harold can read a faded "RM" on one the packs lying on the boat's floor..

"Thanks again," says Harold.

"No problem. Good luck to you," the round man says, then warns, "And watch out. There's wolves around."

The thin man laughs, "They've been killing all our dogs."

As they pull away, Harold calls after them, "Hey, what lake is this?"

"Little Mahihkan," they say in unison.

With several hours of daylight left, Harold decides to continue as well. Mahihkan Lake proper is just a couple more kilometres, tops. Maybe he can reach the Stone's Throw by nightfall. He'll stick close to the shore, in the lee of the wind. The rain has been intermittent and shows signs of letting up altogether. There's not much else that can go wrong now.

17

Although Dianne does not believe me about Dad, she is perfectly willing to insist that rabbits killed the family car.

I'm still amazed at the gulf between us. Instead of shrinking, it seems to be growing. She has clambered down from her chair and gathered her knitting together.

Like everything else Dianne does, Dianne's knitting seems as impulsive as compulsive. She always has to be doing something. My eyes are caught in the rhythm of her fingers twisting the wool into a fabric. I have no idea what it is going to be, but whatever it is, it'll be a robin's-egg blue.

"Is that wool or polyester?"

"Wool," she says.

"Where from?" I ask.

"Sheep," she says.

"I didn't ask who made it, I asked where it's from."

"It might be alpaca, you know."

"Fuck, Dianne. It's a simple question."

"I knew that'd get a rise out of you. But really, I sheared it right off the sheep myself, then I carded it, spun it and dyed it. It was a thing I did in Quebec."

"Oh, that's where you got your French."

"No, but that's where I got to use it."

"Well, where did you learn it?"

"Why is it such a big deal for you where I learned French?"

"Because you won't tell me."

"How do you know I won't tell you?"

"Well, you *haven't* told me so far, and God knows I've hinted around asking."

"It just hasn't worked its way into the conversation yet."

"Well, here it is, all worked in. Now you can tell me.

Dianne flips the wool she's knitting, rearranging it on her lap. She says nothing, of course, but her fingers work furiously trying to think of what to say.

"I was very happy there," she says.

"Oh, that's nice. Where, Dianne?"

"Does it matter, Denny? Does it really matter to you where I learned French? If I really thought — if I was really convinced it mattered, I'd tell you. But really, I'm not going to tell you because you would find a way to intrude upon my happy memory of a happy time. It belongs to me and I'm keeping it."

"Wow!"

"*Wow* what?"

"Another secret."

"What do you mean?"

"Well, we have several going on now; this one's of a happy time."

"Yes, and a happy place."

"The good ol' days, eh?"

"If you want, yes."

"Sounds sad. You know?"

"Whatever, Denny."

165

"You want to know what? You want to hear something really amazing about me?" I ask.

"You're pregnant," Dianne says, her fingers twitching.

"Whoa!" I laugh. I know it's a joke but where'd it come from? The longer I spend with my sister, the less I know her. "Yeah, that'd be amazing." I say.

"Yes, *really* amazing, not just interesting-amazing. But yeah, tell me 'something really amazing', Denny. I'd love to hear it."

"I'm not over being pregnant yet."

"It's not something you ever do get over."

"I guess you'd know."

"I do."

"I mean with Kirsten."

"I know what you mean. So are you going to tell me this amazing thing or what?"

It suddenly no longer seems important, or more to the point, relevant.

"Oh, it was nothing. I was just going to comment on how happy I was."

"You? Ha!" she snorts.

"Yeah, it's not that funny. I mean, I'm a happy human being — fucked up as I am."

"You're right, Denny — it is amazing."

"And you? I mean now, not the 'good ol' days.'"

Her fingers slow down. Stop.

"You've made me lose count," she says.

"I didn't know you were counting."

"That's what knitting is — counting stitches — four, five, six . . . ."

She checks the pattern and starts again.

166

"So is this a ploy or do I get an answer? Or is it worth answering?"

"Happy enough," she says.

"'Happy enough.' What a strange thing to say. What does that mean? Does it mean you're not happy?"

"It means I'm happy enough. It means, given the circumstances, I'm overjoyed."

"Oh, that's what it means."

"Yes, it means if you weren't so damned uplifting, I'd be ecstatic. I'd feel like dancing."

"Oh, this is my fault?"

"If I was any happier, I'd need sedation."

Her fingers work the blue wool furiously. "You're that unhappy, eh?"

She stops, lays her hands in her lap, and looks at me. It's not that she's surprised at what I've said, it's that I've said it — that it shows. "You hide it pretty well, you know." I try to placate her.

"Whatever you say, Denny." She resumes her knitting.

"I'll tell you a secret. Just between you and me." I drain the last of my teacup, the last of my gin. I know I'll make it through the night, but tomorrow morning I'll walk through water or swim through fire to get to Ennisville for something to replace it.

"I don't think I can handle any more secrets," she says.

"I never thought of it that way."

"What?" she looks up.

"That you having them is just as hard as me not knowing what they are — maybe harder."

"Denny . . . " She shakes her head. "Don't make me lose count — again."

"I will not be drinking anymore tonight."

"Good. You've had more than enough. That's no secret."

"That's not the secret. The secret is I will not be entering the Red Zone tonight."

"I thought it was sepia."

"It goes from the Blue to Sepia to the Red Zone. After the Sepia Zone I start hallucinating dead people. The Red Zone."

"I can hardly wait," she says.

"It's okay. You get used to it after you've been there for a while. That's where I usually am."

"And you're happy there." She looks up from her knitting.

"Oh, yeah, usually."

"Usually."

"Sometimes."

"You're happy there sometimes."

"Occasionally," I admit.

"You really are a sonofabitch." She resumes her knitting. The needles clack.

"I would say so, yes. But happy."

"A happy sonofabitch."

"Occasionally, yes."

"And what makes you *un*happy, Dennis?" She stretches her knitting to its full length, almost the length of her arm. I see now that it is a scarf.

"Who's it for?" I ask.

"This?" she says. "No one in particular. I just make them and give them to Dora's House. It's a form of therapy, Dennis. Something you should consider."

"I have my therapy," I say, raising my empty cup. Glancing at the bottom of it, I see a fly wading across the wet bottom. Where the hell did it come from? How long has it been there? I think of the dead mouse out back. Maggots? Do they mature that fast?

"You're not answering my question, are you?"

I slap the cup upside down on my thigh then lift it. The fly has dislodged and now crawls towards my crotch. It's either too wet or too drunk to fly. I flick it away. "I just think it's kind of obvious. I make me unhappy. Me. It's just amazing, actually. I don't know how to explain it. We have these minds, and then we experience these things that happen to us, and we think about them, and that's what makes us unhappy."

"Thinking about things."

"We feel these things and they change us just a bit. And they pile up, all these bits, and before we know it — hey! We're different, not only different than before, but different from each other. But that's not the obvious part, that's not what makes me unhappy . . . ."

"No, of course not."

"It's the ways that we're the same. That's what makes me unhappy. For all our differences, we are ninety-nine percent the same — genetically speaking our DNA is virtually identical. We concentrate on that one percent that makes us different."

"Are you talking about you and me here?"

"I'm talking about the entire fucking human population."

"One percent, eh?"

"But we're ninety-nine percent the same." The fly is now crawling across the floor occasionally stopping to spin in circles. One of its wings is plastered to its body. I wonder where it's going. I wonder if it has a sepia zone.

Reminds me of me — plastered, with only one wing, going in circles.

"I was doing this gig at this lounge, years ago of course, and it's a very nice place, artsy. You would have liked it. No knives, no blood. The hookers all wear clothes. Anyway, there was this guy at the bar. He had cerebral palsy or something that made him spastic. He was in a wheelchair, and I was playing. He was making these sounds, words I guess, and they were filling the room, like smoke, you know? Vaguely annoying. I wanted to tell him to shut up, but how do you tell a guy with cerebral palsy to shut up?

"Right — you don't.

"Anyway, during my break I go to the can for a piss, and who should come bumping through the door but the guy with CP. Except his wheelchair gets stuck. Seeing as how I am not stuck, I give him a hand. I push him to the urinal, and my guess is that he's drunk — or else why would he get stuck in the door? Right? So, I help him up. I help undo his zipper. He pisses. I help him back into his chair. I help him to the sink. All the while he is making sounds, talking to me. Drooling. I wipe his face; he wipes his hands.

"Then I hear what he is saying.

"'I wa-antto-obe-ea-mu-u-s-i-cian. Why ca-an't-I be-ea mu-usi-cian?'

"What do you say? I mean how do you answer a guy like that? How could he possibly . . . Then it occurs to me. So, why can't he be a musician? What's wrong with that? He can be a musician. He can be whatever the fuck he wants. What makes a musician? What makes me think that I'm a musician?

"You see? This is what makes my unhappy. Was I placed on the planet to be a musician? I don't know that.

You don't, although you have your suspicions — but who knows that? God? And he's not saying, is he?"

"No," says Dianne.

"And it's a damn shame too, because some of us would really like to know."

"Yes,"

"What?"

"No, go ahead. You're on a roll."

"Yes. He keeps it a big secret — of course, 'he' could be a 'she,' right? Keeps that big secret from most of us — with no talent. Unless you're Saint Genesius. You know Saint Genesius? My patron saint — the patron saint of performers?"

"No, but I think you're going to tell me."

"Happiness. Unhappiness. He was good, Saint Gene. He must have been. He had a regular gig in the Roman court, you know, with the Caesars. And he's doing some musical revue, and in the revue is sketch about this dumb Christian ritual where they pour water over someone's head, and, poof! He sees all kinds of light and is holy and all that — he's baptized.

"Saint Gene plays the guy who gets baptized. He gets all wet and the court thinks this is very funny, and they laugh and laugh, 'isn't Gene funny, ha-ha.' But no, he's serious. He actually has converted. He's so turned on by his own performance that he's really into it. The court stops laughing. They tell Gene he can relax any time now. But he can't. He doesn't. He becomes his role. He becomes a religious fanatic. So, they throw him to the lions. A martyr.

"Anyway, that's Saint Genesius. What a jerk, eh? No wonder I'm so screwed up. I mean, look at my patron saint. Did he do the right thing? No, he did the wrong thing, that's why they threw him to the lions — he just thought he was doing the right thing. That's why he's a saint.

"And this makes me unhappy too. I mean, it's depressing. It's stupid. It's like Onion Eyes reading the paper upside down. It's like the guy with CP. It's like me. I mean, that's my life trying to figure out what the hell's the right thing to do."

"I thought it was trying to figure out if you were good enough."

"Well that too."

"What you need is *Le Salon*."

"*Le* what?"

"A place to hang your art in 19th Century France. If it was accepted by the members of *Le Salon*, you made it, you could hang your art there. If you didn't, you maybe were like Jules Holtzapffel and committed suicide. You write suicide notes like, 'The Members rejected me. Therefore I have no talent. I must die.'"

"Yeah, well that's one solution. But what about the twenty-seven club?"

"What?"

"All those at the peaks of their careers who didn't make it past twenty-seven — Hendrix, Joplin, Morrison. There's a ton of them. Rick was twenty-seven, but I don't think it was suicide."

Dianne suddenly begins unravelling her scarf. She yanks yarn an arm's length at a time.

"What are you doing?"

"I made a mistake. I have to go back."

A small lake of yarn and silence settles between us. We contemplate happiness lapping against the black stones of our shores. That's an assumption, of course. I have no idea what's lapping against Dianne's shores. I am no nearer finding out the identity of Jimmy Matheson than I was two months ago and Dave still sits on the counter — a pimp from Pisiw Falls — his ashes intact. We've not discussed what we are going to do with them in any kind of detail.

And I'm out of booze.

"I think we should take off tomorrow."

"What?" she looks up from her yarn, stopping mid yank.

"Dump Dave's ashes and head back home."

"We haven't decided what we're doing with them yet."

"You decide and then let's do it. And then we'll go."

"What's your hurry all of a sudden?"

"We just seem to be hanging out here, getting on each other's nerves and not doing what we came here for."

Dianne is clearly not ready for this discussion. She begins rolling the lengths of yarn in a ball. Considering her words.

"We can't go yet," she says.

"Why not?"

"For starters, we have no car."

"Well as soon as the car is ready."

"And you haven't played your gig at the Cantina."

This makes *me* pause and consider *my* words. "Why are you so keen on my playing at the Cantina?"

"A commitment is a commitment."

"I didn't make the commitment, you did!"

"I made it on your behalf."

"You have an answer for everything, don't you?"

"I do my best."

173

She's worn me down. I've got no more. *No mas.* I can feel myself returning to default mode. Self-pity. "All the big cash that's going to bring in. I can just hear all the applause for a one-handed guitar player."

"Just relax."

"I can't relax. I'm out of booze."

"That's another reason to play your gig. Bob said he'd cover your tab."

"I don't believe you. Bob doesn't even cover his own tab."

"I offered to split it."

"Oh, sure. With who?"

She looks at me and cocks her head slightly to one side as if to say, "enough."

"Okay, as soon as I play my gig." I have no intention of doing this but I say it to put an end to this conversation. I know there's a bus that comes by every day or two. I'll take the damn bus back. I've had it. I'll walk back if I have to.

It is quiet, except for the snapping fire in the room beyond. An occasional flutter of plastic covering the screens rustles in the wind.

Then an unmistakeable "Aaaroooo!" fills the night air as though surrounding the cabin.

Dianne's fingers freeze in place. We look at each other.

"I think he's right outside," she says.

We both rise and try to peer into the night. All we see are our blurred reflections. If I open the door, will I scare it away? Or will it go for my jugular?

I flick off the veranda light and we are able to see no more than shadows. Pinpricks of light dot the near shore, including, of course, the ever present orange glow of the

Stone's Throw. Another howl coats the darkness, a little further away. Then I notice a faint light on the far shore.

"See that?" I point.

"Yeah," says Dianne.

There are no cabins on the far shore.

"Someone's camping there and built a campfire," she says.

"Either that or it's the Mahihkan with its fire."

"Don't be ridiculous," she says. " It's lore. Wolves do not make fire."

"Are you going to use the outhouse?" I ask.

"I think I'll use the potty tonight," she says.

"Lore, eh."

"Yeah, well. The howl was very real. That light is somebody's camp."

Red

18

It was a mistake, Harold thinks, *to leave that fire.* Continuing on is out of the question. His eyesight is bad enough with his glasses, but without them, and darkness coming on, he is blind. He'd hoped to make it all the way to the Stone's Throw Campground. But he can't. The capsizing took far more out of him than he'd thought, and after an hour or so of paddling, he had to pull ashore and set up camp. The good news is that he is actually on the lake.

He has chanced upon a campsite used before; a dark ring of stones surrounds a charred fire pit. In the evening half-light, a level bed of pine needles appears to spread clear and welcoming, and most importantly, it's relatively sheltered and dry.

Within an hour, he has set up his tent beneath the old mother pine and coaxes a small flame from the damp kindling. He shelters it with his body, huddling to fight off the wind. Just when he thinks he's finally succeeded and he straightens up to rest his back, a huge gust knocks him off his haunches onto his butt, and obliterates the flame. A small pathetic wisp of smoke tries to rise but is whisked away in the wind.

Harold glumly retreats to his tent a few feet away.
Here, at least, it'll be calm. Climbing inside, he lays out
his sleeping bag upon the thin piece of foam he uses as a
mattress. He wonders how his two rescuers managed to
build a fire so promptly and with such ease earlier in the
day.

He is decidedly hungry but can't even heat up one of the
packages of soy food product. Besides, it's quickly getting
dark. He comforts himself by knowing that tomorrow he
will feast at the Stone's Throw, fill his face with a double-
loaded hamburger with fries and gravy — piss on the
high blood pressure. Although now that he thinks of
it, the small plastic container that holds his piss pills is
not waterproof and its contents are a murky pink paste.
Maybe he'll forego the gravy. He'll decide when the time
comes. Suffice it to say that he'll fuel up completely before
heading across the lake to his cabin.

Settling fully clothed into his sleeping bag, he cannot
find a suitable place to stretch out. Hidden beneath the
smooth bed of needles, the old pine's roots are near the
surface and they run in ridges and feel like long bony
spines despite his foam mattress. How is this possible,
he wonders? It seemed so smooth when he laid out the
tent. He cannot get remotely comfortable and realizes he's
going to have to move the damn thing if wants to get any
sleep at all.

He has not bothered pegging it — no need with his
weight inside — so all he has to do is crawl outside and
yank it a few feet one way or the other. Every bone in
his body aches and he's sure the left side of his face is
swollen twice its normal size. Ignoring the pain, he opens
the zipper and drags himself outside. It occurs to him that

the mosquitoes are not as bad here, in fact, they seem virtually non-existent. He's thankful for small blessings.

The tent moves easily but now that he's aware of the roots, Harold realizes that they are everywhere and extend beyond the tree's shelter. One corner of the tent now sits over the fire pit, but no harm, it's the smoothest spot.

He stops for a moment, squinting, trying to see what's making the strange sound he's certain he's heard. He cannot see much detail beyond forty feet. He sits splayed-legged on the pine needles like a lost child. *Wings.* He recognizes the sound as that of beating wings. *My raven buddies,* he smiles, still unable to find them with his eyes, but then abruptly turns toward the sound of tapping — like a spoon against a water glass, only thicker, heavier.

There, not five feet behind him in some tall grass, are the pair of ravens. They pay no attention to Harold as their heads alternately bow to the sound of the clinking glass. The thought that comes to Harold's mind is *wedding.* His. Tinkling glasses for the newlyweds' kiss. For a brief moment, Reta's lips.

Harold crawls towards the ravens, and just as he is about to reach them, they heave themselves into the air, parting like a feathered black sea and, with a laughing squawk, flap their enormous wings inches from his ears. He sees the object they were bobbing at with their beaks.

It's a bottle.

Examining it, Harold decides it's a wine bottle. He can tell because although the label has long since disintegrated, the cork is sheathed in a leaden hood — which means it must be old as well because nowadays they use shrink-wrap plastic.

The bottle is also full.

He figures he might as well drink it, then if push came to shove he could sleep on a bed of nails and not give a damn.

If only he had a corkscrew. He doesn't even have one at home — (home? What's that?) — at least not after Reta left. She was the wine drinker in the house. He tried it once and thought it tasted like thin cough syrup, only with bubbles. He'd stick with beer. Pil or Boh, please and thank you.

But he's here and now, crawling back into the tent, in no position to be choosey. He picks away at the cork till he's dug a little hole enabling him to push the remainder into the bottle. He tips it back and tastes the dry, almost bitter, grape flavour that warms its way to his stomach. It's not at all how he remembers the taste. For one thing, it's not sweet, nor is it fizzy. He spits the bits of cork that came with it, and this time has a much fuller swig. He'll probably pass out sooner than later because he is not only exhausted, he's barely eaten in two days.

Soon enough, darkness fills the tent and he cannot see how much wine is left in the bottle. He doesn't care though; he's found a comfortable seam between the roots and he is well on the way to being "well-lubricated" as he likes to call this state of inebriation. He clutches the bottle close to him for fear of spilling it. The only problem is his bladder — he has to piss.

As he drinks, it seems Harold must relieve himself every ten or fifteen minutes. This is no fun at all because he barely gets arranged so that the roots are not digging into his hips and back when he has to crawl outside again and do his business. He hangs onto the bottle, though, afraid to set it down in the dark, not only because he might spill it, but because he might not find it in the dark.

Once again he crawls awkwardly across the wet grasses. Clutching the bottle and sleeping bag with one hand, he rises to his feet and takes a few paces towards the lake, unzipping his fly with his free hand. He struggles to pull himself out. It's in there he knows, but much shrunken from the cold and damp.

He holds it and pees into the night. He can't remember when he last used it for purposes other than ridding his body of waste fluids. He can't recall. The only thing he knows for certain is that his partner was Reta. That long ago. How pathetic is that, he wonders?

Stuffing himself back in, he turns to where he thinks the tent should be. However, he can see nothing but a black void on a moonless night. He blinks hard a few times, opening his eyes wide, trying to squeeze some light out of the darkness. He shuffles vaguely in the direction of where he is certain it stands but his face is suddenly clawed by tree branches. The pine — he can smell it. He can also detect a faint scent of smoke. What would possibly be burning now, near here, at this time of night?

Harold turns and backs away from the invisible branches, while a vague glow illuminates the shadows. With absolutely no depth perception, he is unsure if it is nearby or some distance away. He takes a few tentative steps towards it before he is stopped by the fabric of his tent. He realizes the glow is actually coming from within.

Just as he unzips the entrance flaps, the tent erupts into flame. "Fuck!" he says out loud. He can now see that he was wrong to move a corner of his tent atop his attempt at lighting a fire. How is this possible? It certainly didn't look lit.

He tries to reach inside for his pack but the heat turns him away. He stands and tries to beat the flames with his sleeping bag, but steps back and throws the bag on the ground, stomping the flames that have gathered upon it. He shields his face against the heat as his tent flares a brilliant blue then settles into a much more languid but destructive orange-green. Bits of fabric drip in pools of flame, illuminating the skeletal poles that hold little or nothing, like some spiderish creature from another planet.

It's all very pretty in a mesmerizing sort of way; the last bit of his life up in smoke.

Harold laughs.

He drains the bottle he's forgotten to drop, then lobs it into the dregs of the fire.

Across the lake, he hears the unmistakable howl of a wolf.

19

I've been up a couple of hours already and have gotten a fire going — single-handedly. For all my complaining yesterday, the hand does not hurt as much today, but the skin feels tighter. Perhaps because it is now swollen near half again its normal size. There'll be no guitar-playing today, at least not by me.

I'm anxious to leave. I want to go home, even though I don't really have a home to go to. Maybe the paint-shop boys won't have noticed I've been gone. I'll find some way to pay my rent. Maybe pawn Mr. Martin. I'd hate to do that. Maybe there's a cheque waiting in my mailbox, though they've become scarcer and scarcer, fewer and farther between.

I'm going to want a drink in a couple of hours. I'm going to *need* a drink, even if I don't want it. When the fuck am I going to smarten up? Not today. Today will not be a good day for smartening up. But then no day is.

I'm already beyond antsy waiting for Dianne to get the hell out of bed. It's practically eight o'clock. I can spend six hours in bed, max. Then I have to get up or I ache all over. It's the alcohol. It helps you go to sleep in a hurry, but doesn't let you stay that way.

I'm wondering how we're going to get across the lake to Ennisville, to the garage where the Saab is allegedly being fixed. We can't phone because there's no land line here and no cell service. They took the tower down.

I'm thinking we're going to have to row.

I can see Dad's old aluminum boat lying by the shed, upside down, growing some sort of black fungus on the hull. I'm assuming the oars are in the shed. Time to check.

On my way out, I can see that small whitecaps still kick off the grey waves, and above them, near shore, a pair of ravens hang and dip in the wind where they play on an updraft from the bank. On the far shore near the Stone's Throw, something is bobbing in the waves — a log? Too big; it's got to be a boat. In this weather? I need binoculars. I also need keys to the shed. I go back inside.

In the time it's taken me to round the cabin and return, Dianne has risen and is sitting with her knitting as though she's been there all night.

"Welcome to the land of the living," I say.

"A lot you'd know about it," she says without looking up.

Yes, the sooner we get out of here and part company, the better.

"What are you doing?" she asks.

"Looking for binoculars."

"I mean outside," she says.

"Wondering if that boat still floats," I say.

"Apparently, it does," she says.

I have no idea how she might know this and am not going to ask.

"The binoculars are on the counter there, behind Dave." She points with the tops of her needles.

I move the cookie jar and, with some difficulty, get them out of their case.

"What are you looking at?" asks Dianne.

I am now trying to focus through the window, which is hard to do with one hand. Dianne has obviously noticed this and has set down her knitting. She stands beside me. I pass the glasses to her. "I think there's somebody out there. Just in front of the point, towards the Stone's Throw," I say.

She seems to have difficulty at first, finding the far shore. Then she locks in. "My God, you're right," she says, "in a canoe."

"Idiot," I say.

The reason I'm thinking we'll have to row is because the motor pooped out thirty-five years ago and no one has put a wrench to it since, unless it was Dave in a mindless fit of generosity and familial loyalty. But I wouldn't hold my breath. It's a Johnson 9.9 HP that they quit making in the 1970s. It is leaning against the far wall like a drunken cowboy, amid an assortment of broken axes, fish nets, rods, oars, and paddles, as well as heaps of tangled rope, rusted implements, gas cans, and ancient buckets of long-forgotten paints I imagine congealed to rock.

But something is amiss. The motor's clean, so clean it almost shines. It carries none of the grime everything else in the shed wears an abundance of.

Dave has polished it. Of course, he'd have been tickled by the challenge. It would be just like him to fix the goddamn outboard that has not budged from the shed since before Dad died. He would not have done it out of any great love for him, in fact, more the opposite — a safe guarantee of not doing dear old Dad any favours.

From behind the shed, I haul a partially rotted and thoroughly weathered sawhorse to the shed door and mount the motor on it. I hope it won't crumble beneath the weight. I find a fuel tank, remove the cap and take a sniff. Old gas smells like paint. This is fresh — more proof that Dave did some work here — and after priming the motor a bit, I open the choke and give the chord a yank. One pull and it purrs like a kitten at its mommy's tits. I quickly turn it off. I should really have done this in a barrel.

Dianne will be thrilled because she won't have to row. I mean, with my hand and all, she'd insist, and, of course, I'd let her.

Still, it's an unexpected gift from Dave. He always was full of surprises — the bastard. The pimp.

Lugging the motor to the remnants of the dock, which is a couple of posts angled out of the water like a pair of rotting teeth, I bang my shin on the propeller. The new pain is a sharp unwelcome alternative to the throb in my left hand. If I wasn't already awake, I certainly am now. Awake and grumpy. I take no pleasure in tugging and dragging the aluminum boat through the bushes with one hand. Although it isn't heavy, it's certainly awkward. By the time I've hauled the gas can down and attached the motor to the stern, I'm sweating like a pig. This is the most physical exertion I've expended since . . . since the days when I lugged my gigging gear in and out of my one-night stands in two-bit bars back when I did them.

In the old days, I would have sat down and had a smoke now. But I don't do that anymore. One vice is bad enough. Instead, I climb back up towards the cabin on what's left of the overgrown path and meet Dianne on her way down. She is not wearing any pants, in the traditional sense, but those things that look like tights. I'm not sure why but they make me nervous. In one arm, she cradles Dave in his cookie jar, while my guitar case dangles from the other. She has found an old plaid jacket of Dad's, its sleeves so long they hide her hand to give the appearance that the case is directly attached to her arm. It would seem Dianne has made some decisions and that we are leaving directly.

"I was watching you," she says. "I assume you were coming up to get me." She hands me the guitar.

"I can't play this, you know," I say. "And why aren't you wearing any pants?"

"You played it last night, you can play it today," she says, pushing by me. "These *are* pants, Dennis."

"They look like long underwear," I say.

"They are yoga pants."

I follow behind. I'm thinking the folks at the Stone's Throw aren't real used to seeing women in their underwear. I am sucked into the vortex. I'd object, but there's nothing to object against. I want to go to town; I want Dianne's car to be fixed; I want to leave. I am puzzled as to why I feel I am being forced into this.

"What if the car's not ready?" I ask.

"Then we'll take the boat back, won't we?"

I want to argue with her; I want to tell her I'm going back to the city, that I've had enough and that she can take the boat back on her own if she wants because I'm waiting for the bus.

But I won't. I'll require too much effort. Where would I go? And with what? My bag is still here and the little I own inside of it resting on the bed I've been using in the cabin. I know I'm coming back to the cabin even if the car is ready (what would I do, steal it?) because I'm too big of a coward to do anything else.

I manage to keep my mouth shut until we are underway. I very nearly hit the big black rock we swam to and dove from as kids. It looks so much smaller now. I wonder at that, at how things look smaller when you're older, but perplexed that the same rule does not seem to apply to the cabin, at least not in the same way. It does look smaller from the outside, but is somehow larger inside, and the path to the dock is definitely longer than when we were ten.

The small boat jars stiffly against the waves, sending a small spray to each side of the bow. Some of it spits back at us — at me, really. Seems to miss Dianne. It's cold on the water and I'm wishing I had Dave's leather jacket now to knife against the wind. Dianne keeps her chin high, leading with it, spoiling for a fight. She hasn't said anything about the ashes but she clutches them nevertheless, hugging the cookie jar close to her, like she's trying to keep it warm — or maybe for it to warm her.

I'm glad for the all the racket the little Johnson 9.9 makes. Saves me the trouble of having to speak.

The entrance to the Stone's Throw Marina is bridged by a small catwalk, the purpose of which is not entirely obvious — it looks more decorative than practical — until passing beneath it. I see a small video camera strategically angled at the centre of the passageway, eliminating any possibility of anyone sneaking in (or out) of the marina without paying their dock fees, which pretty well explains why it's empty except for a red canoe rocking in the waves tethered to a slip. There is a mighty scrape along one side and I think about the idiot we saw paddling earlier and I wonder if it's his.

"I'll meet you at the cantina," Dianne says as she hands me the cookie jar and clambers ashore. I pass it back to her and she heads up Main Street to the garage. I ponder Mr. Martin sitting in the bottom of the boat and decide I'd better take him along, not because I'm planning to play but because . . . you just don't leave guitars sitting in the bottom of boats. I haul it out and head for the Cantina. I feel silly, though, lugging the guitar. I need a drink.

One wall of the cantina actually faces the marina giving a view of the lake, except that the bars over the windows give it a vaguely menacing look and make you wonder if they are to keep people out, or keep them in. There's a fire door there as well that looks like it's never been opened, and leaning against the wall next to it is a canoe oar. I'm thinking the owner of the canoe has parked it there.

Even when it was brand new, the Stone's Throw Cantina was makeshift and shabby. Old man Ennis must have bought all the furniture used. Mixed and mismatched, the speckled Formica-topped tables were invariably scarred with worms of shit-coloured cigarette burns. Some sat on single-stemmed, cast-iron legs, others had four. They all managed to wobble because the floor was uneven. The metal-framed plywood chairs were bent and uncertain. That's how I remember it, and the big, square room hasn't improved an iota or changed much except for the bank of VLTs half hidden by a two-thirds high wall, blinking and winking like an alien army ready to take your money and take your mind. Send it all back to the mother ship. Taxidermied fish and animal heads sporadically poke through the walls. A stuffed owl clutches a stuffed squirrel on a tree stump. A large bear stands near the door. The bear is holding a cup. The sign on the cup says, "Tip me." It is predictably full of bottle caps and cigarette butts. No one has tried to take the sign literally because the bear is still standing. Its stuffed feet are screwed into the floor.

I'd forgotten about the garish green hue lent to everything — the result of fluorescent lighting mixed with railroad-station green walls, a colour you don't see much anymore and one that nobody misses. Even though tobacco smoking has been outlawed in all public places for years, the place still reeks of eau d'ashtray. The pool table felt is nearly worn down to the slate and large beer stains show the contour of the slope the table shouldn't have.

In one corner, next to the fire exit, is a small raised platform — a stage — where you could stuff a three-piece band provided you set the speakers on the floor. Presently it is occupied by a karaoke machine sitting on a chair plugged into a flat-screen TV monitor that hangs on the wall. A naked black mic stand with a gleaming chromium head occupies centre stage. It looks alien — to the room and to the planet. A sign hangs from its neck.

I walk closer. Written in felt pen, in the same hand that wrote "Tip Me" on the bear, it says, "Live music today. Denny Givens. *Hiding*."

Fuck.

I've barely sat down when four guys walk in. They're clearly already pissed and ready to take on the night, except it's not even mid-afternoon. I turn my back on them and focus on Mr. Martin's case, arranging it so that it's easy to open, should I decide to do so. I stare at it. It's loaded with decals from various places it's been, the highlights of my touring life — Upper Shediac Falls, Truro, Moncton, Smiths Falls, Wawa, Red Deer — all the big places, centres of cultural vibrancy. It also sports several commercial labels, guitar makers like Yamaha and Ibanez even though I've never owned either. In the old days, there was prejudice against "Nip" guitars as they were called, and the decals were a kind of mask for Mr. Martin. However, they tell me that some of these Japanese companies have business plans that extend for five hundred years. Boggles the mind. I doubt that Martin has a five hundred-year business plan. I doubt the four assholes arguing about pool cues have a five *minute* business plan. But then, I should talk.

"You must be Denny," a voice startles me from behind. I turn and it's the devil himself — Bobby Ennis. He looks just like his dad who used to sell me off-sale when I was a kid, with the same cocaine nose and rheumy eyes. With my guitar case perched on a chair across from me, it's going to be difficult to deny who I am.

"Yeah, well, you can see I've had an accident." I indicate my bandaged hand. "I won't be able to do much." I hadn't planned on doing anything. I feel ambushed.

"Can I get you something? Coffee? Pop? Beer?" He's covering all the bases. He doesn't want to risk offending me.

"Gin," I say. "Neat is good. Make it a double."

"Right ho," he says and saunters back towards the bar, which, compared to the rest of the room, is bright and cheery — and well-stocked. I will not leave here without drinking at least one of those blue bottles and taking another home with me.

I open Mr. Martin's velvet-lined coffin. I might as well tune the damn thing. I should be able to fake my way through a set in open C. I have my capo if I think I need to change keys. I struggle to snake a pick out of my pocket.

Aside from the four yahoos at the pool table, two or three seniors are at the VLTs rendering their pension cheques unto the mother ship. One lonely old guy eats a plate of fries like they are his last meal. He looks like he just stumbled in from the bush. He could do with an introduction to a razor and a bar of soap. I wish I had his hair though — a full head of silver. He looks up at me and squints, then goes back to his plate. He's had a run-in with something nasty on the left side of his face. I think of the scrape on the canoe and wonder if it's his. He swills the last of a Pilsner to help wash down the fries and hollers at Bob to bring him another one.

I take an instant dislike to him.

Above the bar I notice a monochrome video screen. It's a security monitor. It alternates various views of the Stone's Throw property. One of them is the entrance to the marina.

And then it comes to me, "Water, water, flowing free / Underneath the bridge to sea . . . "

I can't find a pencil fast enough.

20

After Harold polishes off the greasy hamburger, he starts in on the greasy fries. He can almost feel his arteries clogging, but hey, this is a celebration; he's reached his goal, well, almost, just a short jaunt across the lake to his cabin. He cannot remember when food tasted so good which is exactly what he thought two nights before when he sat in the trapper's cabin in the rain. Washing the fries down with a beer makes it all that much better.

He isn't quite done when a balding man with a ponytail walks into the cantina. He is somewhat paunchy and carries a guitar case. Harold thinks he might be in his mid-fifties, a bit younger than him. His left hand is heavily bandaged. Harold watches Ponytail Guy navigate through the room as though he is trying to remember where he is. He stops in front of the stage, sets down the guitar and reaches towards the mic stand, grasping a small sign that hangs from it.

He hears the man utter a short "fuck."

Harold assumes he is the musician Bobby Ennis has told him about. For a second, their eyes meet. There is something vaguely familiar about Ponytail Guy but Harold is without his glasses and unable to grasp the fine details of his face. So not wanting to stare or, more correctly, get caught doing so, he turns away and orders another beer from Bob in a voice that seems to belong to someone else. He startles himself.

"Right," says Bobby, annoyed. "I hear ya."

He wonders where the waitress is who used to work here. She never took any bullshit from anyone but still managed to smile and make you feel welcome anyways. Plus, she could handle eight or ten beer on a tray with no trouble at all. He is kind of amused watching Bobby run around the bar with one drink at a time.

Ponytail Guy has set his guitar case on a chair and Harold can study him now that his back is more or less to him. He knows he's met him before but just can't place where. Or when. He's amused the way Ponytail Guy stares at his case, like maybe it's a ticking bomb and he's a sapper trying to figure out how to defuse it. It's like he's in a trance and he jumps when Bobby approaches to take his order — a double something. Then, a bit later, Harold sees Ponytail Guy writing on his guitar case.

The cantina door suddenly bangs open and three scruffy young men try to enter at the same time. They are pushed through by a fourth, their obvious leader, a man with dirty blond hair and no cartilage in his nose. They are loud and bored and looking to get drunk quickly.

"Hey, my man, four of your best Bud," the leader announces, "to *drink*," he emphasizes, laughing. The others laugh too.

Harold doesn't get the joke.

"Charlie here is paying," the leader slaps Charlie's back. Charlie is the most respectable looking of the lot. He's probably the one with a job. "Fuck off, Lee," he says.

Harold knows that if Charlie wasn't actually buying the beer, he'd never tell Lee to fuck off, because no one in his right mind would tell a guy like that to fuck off. He wonders if Lee is his first name or last. He wouldn't want to meet him in a dark alley, that's for sure. He wouldn't want to meet him anywhere, for that matter. Still, he can hardly take his eyes off him. He's never seen a man with a nose like that before, like a caricature of a boxer, an Irish boxer Harold decides.

Harold notices Bobby Ennis glance at the four settling around the pool table as he serves him. *Potential trouble,* is probably what he is thinking.

"Thanks," says Harold. "What happened to that gal who used to work here?"

"Barb? She's still here. Took the day off though. I think her boyfriend is back from Fort Mac. I could sure use her today."

Bobby continues on to Ponytail Guy, waiting for his double-something. Vodka, or gin? It's clear, whatever it is.

"So, at least you got an audience," Bobby says, indicating the four newcomers, two of whom are rolling pool cues on the table, trying to find the straightest — like it would make a difference in their games. "That'll be eight-fifty."

Harold watches the Ponytail Guy's jaw drop and knows he's probably thinking *Eight-fuckin-fifty?* But he answers, "Put it on my tab — or Dianne's. She'll be here soon." Whoever Dianne is. His girlfriend, he guesses, or maybe his wife.

At the pool table, Lee slips a loonie into the slot and pulls the release. The balls rumble through invisible alleys within the table to a port at one end where he gathers them up and sets them upon the threadbare felt.

"Who wants to get beat first?" he says.

"Sure," says Charlie, getting to his feet.

"For a beer, eh," says Lee.

"I'm already getting your fuckin' beer."

"Two, then."

"What if I win?"

"You only have to buy me one."

Harold watches this, thinking if he has a couple more beers, he might challenge the table himself. He used to play a bit of pool when he was a kid. Got pretty good at it too, although that was long ago, even before he met Reta. Still, he'd play the odd time on long hauls, in the evening when he got too tired to drive but wanted to unwind a bit before he hit the sack.

"What are you looking at, Mashface?" Lee is talking to Harold.

"Huh? Nothing, nothing," says Harold. He must have been staring. He turns away and studies the stuffed owl clutching the stuffed squirrel. A couple more beers, he thinks, and he'll take 'em on, the asshole. He didn't paddle all the way to Mahihkan Lake for some jerk to call him Mashface.

He chugs his beer before rising to go to the bar for another. He has hardly taken a step when a great rush of dizziness overcomes him and he quickly sits back down. His first thought is that he's missed taking his piss pills, maybe that's the cause. On the other hand, he has just drained an almost full bottle of beer — that has to be accounted for as well. Plus, he didn't get a lot of sleep under his canoe after his tent burned down. *Take it easy,* he tells himself. Maybe he should just leave. He is caught between renting one of Bobbys Ennis' cabins at the

Stone's Throw Campground and RV Park, or sucking it up and paddling across the lake to his own cabin. Two more hours, he guesses, in a bit of wind is all it would be. The rain has pretty well stopped. But maybe a night's sleep in a dry bed, a real bed, would go a long way to rejuvenating a man.

Because money is tight, he is leaning towards the two-hour paddle when the cantina door opens and in walks a woman straight out of a fashion magazine — a real looker, with straight black hair tumbling halfway down her back like a midnight waterfall. She is wearing a pair of black leotards, black red-laced hiking boots, and a red and black plaid lumberjack jacket. Even Harold can see this is colour coordination of an extremely high order. The only odd thing is that she is toting what looks like a cookie jar. Harold can tell by the big red smiley-faced strawberry painted on the jar. *What the hell is she doing here?*

She takes a quick glance around, ignoring the ogling eyes of the boys at the pool table, and marches directly across the room to the Ponytail Guy. There, she plunks the cookie jar on the table where the balding musician is now tuning his guitar and an intense rapid-fire monologue follows. Harold can hear words like "car" and "ashes" and "cabin." The musician occasionally responds with shrugs and monosyllabic murmurs. *It must be his wife*, thinks Harold. He does hear the phrase "Eight-fifty?" loud and clear. It's her voice, dark and velvety, a twilight voice. When Harold was younger and forty pounds lighter, he might make himself a little more apparent than he presently is, hunched over his beer. He might sit up, smile, and nod. You never know. Forgetting himself for a moment, he straightens. "Bobby, can you bring me another?" Harold tries not to yell. His decision is made. He's staying. He holds his near-empty Pil aloft to indicate what he wants.

Bobby has stopped to stare at the woman as well. He turns to Harold and nods.

Like a flash of unexpected lightning, Lee jumps the cue ball off the table. It lands with a loud bang and rolls crackling across the floor. It hits Harold on the foot. His startled reaction — a reflex, really — boots the ball to the other end of the room, towards the musician and the woman where it stops at her feet.

She bends over and picks it up. She holds it aloft, cradling it in the palm of her hand like an egg on a teraspoon.

For a moment, everything is still, then Harold watches the woman slowly close her hand around the ball, take her arm back and whiz it across the room at the pool-table guys who scatter like a school of minnows.

21

Water, water flowing free / Underneath the bridge to sea
Water, water, flowing free / Take him far away from me.

I can't write it down fast enough. It's a start, or maybe an end — I don't care. It's how they all come. In fits and starts, in no particular order, and when you least expect it. Then the phrasing. The phrasing is as important as the melody. I doesn't matter what it means, just how it sounds. That's what music is — sound — sound and silence, measured and pitched.

I barely lift my pen from where I've been writing (the Suzuki label on my guitar case) when Dianne traipses in like Lady Macbeth, all red plaid, black underwear, and about ready to rub out the damned spots. I can tell the news is not going to be good.

"The car is not ready," she confirms. They don't know *when* the part will get here. They recommend I *ship* it home to the dealer. Fuck!" she says. "How do you ship a fucking car?"

I just assume this is a rhetorical question. I certainly don't know the answer. She plunks poor Dave upon the table and looks around. Every eye in the place is still on her, or was till she takes them all in.

"What the fuck are they staring at?" she says.

Now this I know the answer to.

"You're not wearing any pants," I say.

"Oh fuck off," she says. "These cost me a hundred and thirty bucks and I have the brand name to prove it."

"I don't think yoga fashion has made it here yet. And I don't think I've ever heard you swear before."

"I'm pissed off," she says, stating the obvious. "I don't know whatever possessed me to come up here."

She doesn't add, "with you," but I know it's there. And she knows the reason as well as I do, better I suspect. I tap the cookie jar with my pen.

"Yeah, yeah, yeah — the fucking ashes, the fucking cabin . . . the whole thing."

I have never heard her like this.

"And *you* swilling away like a goddamn fish."

"This is my first," I say, defensively. "Two ounces is not very swilling, especially at eight-fifty a pop."

"Eight-fifty!" she screeches.

"I told Bob that you were covering my tab."

"Cover your own fucking tab! I've had it with covering tabs. If it's not yours, it's Kirsten's; if it's not Kirsten's, it's Steve's. I'm always picking up someone's tab. It's time someone covered *my* tab for a change. You can stay here and wash dishes to cover your fucking tab."

I consider life as a dishwasher for a fraction of a second and know instinctively I would be no good at it and that I would be fired before my first shift was over.

"Okay," I say. "Whatever you say."

"Don't say 'whatever' to me!"

"I certainly won't," I say. "Never again." Now is not the time to antagonize her.

201

A huge bang erupts from the pool table and a ball explodes across the room, pinballing off the old guy and a half dozen tables and chair legs all the way to Dianne's feet, where it comes to a thoughtful rest.

She gazes at it for a second then picks it up, as though it is Yorick's skull and she's about to deliver a soliloquy. Instead, she slowly closes her hand around it, folds it into her chest, then wings it across the room like a baseball pitcher. I'm amazed at the form, and her penchant for throwing things. The guys at the pool table scatter like pigeons. One of them actually yelps.

She hits the stuffed bear square in the "Tip Me" cup. It explodes a generous mix of bottle caps, cigarette butts, and bubble gum wrappers. There is a moment of silence. Then one of them speaks.

"What the fuck was that about, lady?" The man who is asking the question carries a pool cue. He is missing most of his nose, or the cartilage to support it. Although he and his cohorts are on the other side of the room, I can see they want to have a closer meeting

"All right! Everyone settle down!" Bobby commands like a man wielding a double-barreled shotgun. Except he's not.

"That broad winged the cue ball at us," says No-nose.

"Then keep the damn thing on your table!" Dianne says. She is still standing in her baseball-pitcher pose.

The old guy is sitting halfway between us and them, squinting like he's half blind, snapping his head back and forth. He's holding his beer in front of his face but can't find time to take a sip. Even one of the VLT junkies has stopped for a moment to check out the action. It's free. Beats losing a buck every three seconds.

This could get ugly. It is clear that something has gotten into Dianne beyond not knowing how to ship a car, and that whatever it is, it seems to have left her quite capable of provoking violence. There will either be blood or a quick exit, possibly both. I, of course, would prefer the quick exit.

Trouble is, I don't have any booze. I will have to stick around for a bit longer.

"Don't tell me where to keep my balls, sweetheart," says No Nose.

A couple of sniggers erupt from the peanut gallery.

"You don't have any balls, asshole," retorts Dianne.

I've got to admit that I'm with Dianne's assessment of No Nose being an asshole, and I even support the sentiment, but it is normally one you keep to yourself even if you have to bite your tongue.

However, this has not happened and the tension index, if there is such a thing, has risen to the point where something is going to break.

All eyes widen. Breathing stops.

Bobby ducks behind the bar.

He suddenly stands up with a double-barrel shotgun levelled on the counter.

"Okay. Party's over. This bar is closed! Everybody out! Starting with you four. You get in whatever got you here and get out," he says, now setting the stock of the gun on the counter, the barrels pointing at the ceiling. You got to hand it to Bobby; the gun might even be loaded. "She threw the fucking cue ball!" says No Nose.

"Who shot the thing across the room and hit me in the leg!" she screams. Then continues, "In fact, it hit *two* people. Right sir?" she says to the old guy.

He nods briefly. Then sips his beer staring straight ahead.

"Aw fuck off. That happens all the time, and it was barely rolling when it got to you," says No Nose, taking a step towards us.

A large *ca-chunk* emanates from the bar, the sound of a twelve-gauge shotgun shell sliding into its chamber.

"All right. Out. All of you. Now. Before I accidentally pull this trigger." Even though he says *all of you*, he is clearly referring to No-nose and his three amigos. You can tell by how he doesn't take his eyes off them.

They all shuffle towards the door. You can hear their feet crunching on the ashes and bottle caps. As they exit the doorway, No Nose delivers a parting shot. "Why don't you wear some fucking clothes, you fucking whore!"

Quietly, maybe to herself, Dianne says, "They're Lululemon," and slumps into a chair. Her face contorts into a tragic mask. "I called home from the garage. Kirsten has disappeared again," She starts sobbing. "I'm such a great fucking mother."

Bobby has gone outside, still toting the shotgun, most likely to make sure the magnificent foursome has indeed departed. There is some muffled shouting before vehicle doors slam followed by the roar of something large — a truck maybe, or a tank — its diesel engine grinding away, idling in annoyance. It does not leave, however.

I have no idea if Dianne is a good mother or not. She didn't have a hell of a good role model in our mother, and one grandmother died before she was born, the other shortly after.

Dianne is sobbing convulsively. Comforting people has never been my strong suit. I do the brotherly thing — I pat her on the back in a weak attempt to soothe her.

She shakes me off. "I don't need burping!" she manages to snap and blubber at the same time.

Pulling my hand away, I am suddenly aware of another presence. The old guy is hovering behind us. I look at him, and he shrugs as if that is some kind of explanation for his being there.

"I know how she feels." He says it to me by way of clarification, I guess. He has a soft, soothing voice — the voice of a priest — and while he can't possibly have any inkling as to how Dianne feels, she turns to him and says, "Thank you."

I get shaken off; the stranger gets thanked.

The angry idling continues growling outside, like the boys are sitting in their tank deciding what to do while Bobby stands guard. I don't know if he's protecting us or holding us prisoner.

Time for me to go meet an old friend in a blue glass jacket. I get up from the table leaving Dianne with the stranger. He does not look nearly as old up close, and although considerably beat up, he is only a year or two older than me at most.

I cross the room to the bar, and from behind it, I pull down an almost full forty ouncer of Bombay Sapphire then head straight to the fire escape. I open the door and set the bottle outside next to it. Returning to the table, I see the old guy and Dianne are in some kind of conversation.

"I hate to break up your party here, but it's time for us to leave," I say, picking up my guitar.

"Harold is coming with us," says Dianne.

I'm thinking, *fuck, they're already on a first-name basis*, but say, "Whatever," instead.

"He's going to paddle over," Dianne adds. "He doesn't have a place to stay."

This stops me. I turn and look at them. It has obviously been decided no matter my response, but I am wondering what's wrong with the campground or one of Bobby's cabins. I nod, then turn, heading for the fire door. I hear more shouting from beyond the main entrance, then a huge fucking bang.

I'm hoping it's the truck back firing but I know it's the shotgun.

22

Harold is thoroughly impressed by the beautiful woman's cue-ball fling and wishes his reflexes had been quicker so that he could have done the same thing, but knows deep down he would never have had the nerve.

During the brief standoff between her and Lee, he is even more impressed, but is nevertheless wondering about his escape route options should this break into a fully fledged barroom brawl, and so is grateful when Bobby suddenly shows up with a shotgun to usher the thugs out of the building.

He can now focus all his attention on the beautiful woman with the great arm and nerves of steel. His semi-clogged arteries have skipped a beat or two in all the excitement. He becomes confused and concerned as he watches the beautiful woman folded over the table shuddering with giant sobs.

It's the shock, he thinks — there can be no sadness here. She cannot be weeping with grief; she is weeping at the sudden passing of danger. He recognizes this as similar to when Reta left him. He had cried then and knew his were not tears of grief or sorrow, for he had hated her then and could not wait for her to be gone. Tears of relief is what he had decided, then.

He finds himself standing behind them as she shrugs off the arm of Ponytail Guy who simultaneously turns and looks up at him.

"I know how she feels," says Harold.

Ponytail guy's mouth opens but no sound comes out. Instead, the beautiful woman turns to him and says, "Thank you."

Now that he is close to them, they both look familiar and he is certain he has seen them before but cannot for the life of him remember where or when.

Ponytail guy abruptly gets up and marches across the room. Harold takes this as an opportunity to sit down and make himself acquainted with the beautiful woman who acknowledges him by attempting to dry her eyes on the sleeves of her plaid jacket.

"I thought you were very brave," he says.

"Not really," she says, tugging at the end of a sleeve to make it cover her wrist with which she wipes her nose. "I just lost control."

"I was still pretty impressed," he says. "I'd buy you a drink but I don't think your boyfriend would like it."

"My boyfriend? God, no! He's my brother!" she laughs.

Then it hits him. Harold remembers when he was a kid there was a family in a cottage not too far from his in the Cove. He remembers the sign going down their lane which they had to pass going to their place that read, "Givens Gulch." There were boys and a little girl. One of the boys was an Indian — a red-headed Indian — which probably meant he was a half-breed, which meant he was a welfare kid.

This was a problem.

Harold's mother believed you couldn't trust people who took in welfare kids. Those kind of people had no scruples about how they made their money — how else could you explain a family with two white kids and an Indian? Even if the Indian was a half-breed, it was the same thing except maybe worse because somebody, sometime, knew better. And to make matters worse, the Indian kid used to run around naked. Well, once anyway.

It's not that Harold actually recalls any of his mother's musings exactly, only that he wasn't allowed to go play with that set of neighbours even though he would watch from a distance and hear their incessant whoops and hollers splashing about a big black rock in front of their cabin. He could not see what his mom objected to because they certainly seemed to be having a good time.

The Indian kid had a slingshot that Harold lusted after, especially after watching him knock a herring gull off the black rock all the way from shore. Harold had three dollars saved — his exhibition money — and breaking his mother's rule of boycotting the family, offered all three dollars to the Indian who accepted the deal on the spot. He remembers the kid's ear-to-ear grin as he tried to say something but only stuttered instead.

But in a peculiar turn of events, Harold lost the slingshot the very next day. He could not find where he had hidden it despite being positive it was behind a certain tree, beneath a certain rock, and he could not tell his mother about it because that would be admitting he had broken one of her cardinal rules. And then he later had to lie about what happened to his savings, saying he'd spent it on firecrackers which he had in fact wanted to do anyway, and for which he was grounded during exhibition week. But still, the slingshot had simply vanished.

The only odd thing was that he still saw the Indian kid with a slingshot that, from a distance at least, looked remarkably like the one he had bought off him.

After that, Harold was more diligent about listening to his mother's warnings. For a while, anyway, until he met Reta who offered a whole new set of rules. But they're both gone now, his mother long since dead, and Reta, well, who knows.

"Are you one of the Givenses?" asks Harold.

"Yes, I'm Dianne," says Dianne, surprised.

"I'm Harold Huckaluk." Harold extends his hand. "You have that place on Real Point?"

"Yes," says Dianne again, looking hard at Harold now, trying to place him.

"You wouldn't remember me, but we have a place not too far past you — at the Cove?" his framing it as a question suggests that Harold hopes she might remember it if she tries hard.

But all that Dianne knows is that "the Cove" and most its structures went up in smoke a year ago.

"It's gone," she blurts.

"What's gone?" asks Harold.

My God! He doesn't know, thinks Dianne. However, she is flustered now and does not know what else to say, so blurts again, "the Cove!"

"Yes — I guess that's progress," Harold smiles. He thinks that Dianne is referring to the rate and pace of development, especially with the new golf course, and how things have changed over the years, even though he himself has not been near Mahihkan Lake more than a handful of times since Reta left, the last being at least a couple of years ago. He is happy to have this conversation with the beautiful woman, Dianne Givens, from his childhood, even though she doesn't seem to be able to remember him.

Instead of informing this poor old guy, Harold Huckaluk and his chewed-up face, that his cabin is likely no more than a mound of ashes, Dianne decides it would be best to ease him into it. "You must come visit us, soon, in case something has happened to your place; you're welcome to stay with us. There was fire over in the Cove last year and some of the cabins were destroyed."

Harold is overwhelmed by this generosity and isn't quite sure what to make of it. "I'd have to paddle," he says, trying to make a joke. The "us" she refers to must be her and her musician ponytail brother — the *Hiding* singer, who hurries by them to the fire exit, opens it for a moment, bends over, then straightens up and closes the door.

"Weren't there three of you? I mean, like, wasn't there two boys and you?"

"Yes," says Dianne. "He's right here." She pats the cookie jar. "His ashes," she adds.

"Oh! I'm sorry."

"Not to worry," says Dianne.

The musician has made his way back to the table.

"I hate to break your party up, but I think it's time for us to leave," he says pointedly to Dianne.

"Harold is coming to visit us," says Dianne. "He's going to paddle over."

"Whatever," says her brother as he picks up his guitar case, apparently in a big hurry.

Harold and Dianne rise. They all glance towards the main entrance from where renewed shouting occurs — followed by the explosion of a twelve-gauge shotgun.

Harold can tell what it is from his days as a hunter.

23

We hurry to the boat, I am thankful again for Dave's mechanical abilities. The old engine starts again on the first pull. I feel like we're on the lam for murder. Maybe we are. Accessories after the fact.

Dianne is sitting near the bow with Dave, intent on watching behind me as Harold gets his canoe going. The wind has calmed, which, I'm told, typically means it is changing directions. We can just boot it as fast as these 9.9 horses will go, but Harold will just have to hope it doesn't come up a gale against him, or worse, across him.

But what do I care, really?

Nothing.

Back at the cabin, there is nothing but a terrible silence. We are both of us locked in our solitudes. I'm not sure which is worse, the threat that we will stay there, or the threat that we will emerge. The ashes issue has not been broached. Dianne knits. I poke at a fire I've begun. I'm assuming that we'll be busing out of here tomorrow but that is only an assumption. Perhaps we'll be escorted out by Canada's finest beneath red and blue flashing lights.

In the evening light, my bottle of stolen booze is a paler blue than the sapphire it is meant to represent. It sits on the counter next to Dave in the cookie jar. The big red strawberry glistens. A fly buzzes by my ear and sits on the strawberry. Disappointed, it buzzes off and beats its head against the window. I know exactly what it feels like.

The wind has perked up again, and throws a draught of smoke back through the stove. It smells strangely of burning flesh. Perhaps a bit of wool has reached the stove. I finger a strand of it and am surprised by its coarseness.

"Don't touch that," Dianne says. Her first words to me since the cantina.

"Oh, hello! She speaks."

"I don't want you touching anything of mine," she says.

"Okay, it's a deal. You stay away from my gin, I'll stay away from your wool." Refilling my cup, I see the fly is still trying to break out. If the window wasn't painted shut, and I had use of both hands, I'd open it to let him out. Instead, I try to put him out of his misery with my thumb.

"Leave that alone too," she says.

"You don't own the fucking fly, Dianne." I'm surprised by my tone. It's a bit nastier than intended.

Dianne suddenly sets down her knitting and rises. She starts towards her bedroom, or the one she's claimed as hers, our parents' room.

"Where are you going?" I ask.

"I think I'll go bury Dave now. Then I'm going to pack up what I can carry and head to the Throw, where I will get a room tonight and then catch the bus from tomorrow morning. That is where I am going."

"What about your buddy, Harold? He's paddling his ass off across the lake to rescue you — or are you rescuing him?"

"You know what, Denny? He's a big boy just like you. He can figure out a way to take care of himself." She disappears into the bedroom.

"Dianne. I'm sorry. Don't go."

She reappears at the doorway, folding something — socks?

"You're not sorry. You don't know how to be sorry. There are holes in you that are so big — I've had enough. I give up. You can stay here till it's sold, then I don't care what you do. You can go live under a bridge. Have a *really* nice life." She turns back into the room.

That echo from Twyla's note reminds me that if I lose my sister, I will truly have nothing. *You don't know what you have till it's gone.* In the failing light and rising wind, I can see Harold halfway here. I hope the poor sonofabitch makes it. I don't know him or anything about him, but he is clearly smitten by my little sister.

The fly suddenly leaves the window and rises to the now-dominant source of light in the kitchen, a bare incandescent light bulb above the sink. It seems to hover near it like a hummingbird. Then I realize it is caught in a web. A spider suddenly appears as if out of nowhere, but know it must have been there all along. In seconds, it wraps the fly in a kind of webby gauze. I have never witnessed this before. The insect still buzzes, struggling. But it is doomed.

I debate setting it free, but what would that accomplish — more maggots. I will leave things as they are. I will wish Dianne a fond farewell and be done with it. Except I have one more question.

"How come you and Dave could fly?" I have not said this very loud. In fact, I am surprised by the sound of my voice.

Dianne, too, is surprised. She emerges again from the bedroom.

"Just you and Dave floating around the ceiling. And I was on the floor watching — how come?

"I don't know, Denny."

"That never struck you as odd?"

"No."

"It sure struck me as odd. So how did you do it?"

Dianne doesn't want to have this conversation. She turns to go back to the bedroom.

"No, no, no. You can't leave till you answer me that. Then you can go, hitchhike, walk, take the bus — whatever you're going to do. I mean, you're right. I have holes in me you can drive a truck through, or a bike through. But they're not quite empty. They're filled with shadows, and they're dark, and I don't know what's in them — except for questions, and one of them is how you did that. How you and Dave flew around the room. And the reason I want to know is because I couldn't do that. It's not that I was jealous — it's just that I was puzzled. Am puzzled."

"I don't know. I don't remember."

"You don't remember."

"I just remember being there. It was fun. It was the single most exhilarating moment of my life. And then you came in the room . . . You know what you did, eh?"

"I told you to get down. I tried pulling on you but you were hung up there like you were on strings. I was afraid of how you got there. And even more afraid of how Dave did, because I believed in angels then, and that angels could fly. I knew you might be one, but I also knew Dave wasn't. It scared me. It still scares me." I take a drink from my teacup. I don't know why it seems to taste better from a teacup. Maybe it's the shape. I am still standing near the sink, next to the counter. Dave in his strawberry-faced cookie jar smirks up at me. "Fuck! That's how you did it. You did it with strings!"

"There were no strings, Denny."

"Wires then. Dave would do that just to fuck me up! You were just a baby. You wouldn't know any better. That's why he told me to get out. No stutter, Nothing. Clear and distinct. That sonofabitch." I grab the cookie jar, and head to the door. "I'm going to throw him into the lake right now. He can go swim with his ancestors."

"Don't," says Dianne.

I stop at the door and turn to see her holding my guitar — Mr. Martin. She has him over her shoulder.

"There were no wires, no strings. We were flying."

"What the fuck are you doing?"

"Throw those ashes and I'll smash your guitar. I will."

I'm already amazed at how quickly she's removed it from its case. And I've certainly seen her recent penchant for violence. But that involved throwing things. "It's not like you to go about smashing things, Dianne."

"Actually, it is, Dennis. I smash things all the time. My daughter, your niece, smashes things too. That's why I'm so worried about her."

I'm thinking, *Holy shit, my sister is a nutcase!* "But you're not going to smash my guitar."

"Actually, Dennis, if it really was your guitar, I wouldn't. But, you know something? It's my guitar. I paid for it with my own money twenty-five years ago."

I suddenly understand the word "gobsmacked". "I beg your pardon? That was a gift from Dave."

"No. It was a gift from me."

"He said it fell off a truck."

She suddenly swings the guitar around her shoulders , bashing its body against the corner of the stove. Splinters fly everywhere. She lifts it over her head and swings it like an axe a half-dozen more times till all she's holding is the neck and six strings. She tosses them onto the middle of the floor.

I'm still standing in the doorway holding the cookie jar. "Well, okay. You've got my attention. Now what?"

"What the hell am I going to do?" She slumps into a chair.

"About what?"

"Everything. Kirsten."

"Good question, Dianne — what?"

"What's the point?

"What's the point? Is there a point? Listen, I'm down a guitar here. Are you trying to say something? What?"

"I can't."

"Can't what? You seem to be pretty good at expressing a fair amount of rage here and you're saying you can't what?"

"I can't tell you."

"Well then don't. Whatever it is, I've lived this long without knowing, I can manage a few more years till my liver gives out. The real question is where am I going to get another guitar? I'll never own anything as nice as that . . . God." I'm toeing through the debris on the floor. "It was one of the few things I was attached to. And now it's fucking kindling. Thanks, Dianne"

"You remember the letter?"

"What letter?"

"Jimmy Matheson?"

Oh. This is where this is going. I say nothing. I simply look at her.

"He was a little tiny baby boy, twenty-five years ago. I don't know who he is now. He was born in Kelowna. He was born in a town beside a lake, where old people go to die. That's where he was born, and I was his mother. I was twenty. When I went to find out if I was pregnant, the doctor said: 'You've got the disease.' He thought he was making a joke. But it wasn't very funny. And you were in Cape Breton."

"And Dave was in jail."

"Dave was the father."

The cookie jar slips through my arm. I go to catch it with my bandaged hand but merely knock the lid off. The jar hits the floor. The lid flies and shatters. The jar does not break, but tips onto its side spilling ashes among the guitar ruins.

"Fuck," I say.

Dianne disappears into the bedroom.

In the dimming of the day, I'll need more light to clean up this mess. I turn the kitchen light on and glance through the window where I can still make out the solitary figure in the canoe, now about halfway here.

"Fuck!" I scream.

I'm not going to make much of a host when our guest arrives.

I find the broom and start sweeping — a difficult task with only one good hand. Bits of Dave get stuck between the floorboards.

24

Harold is vaguely annoyed that the Givenses did not offer to tow him across the lake but quickly rationalizes that they had no tow rope. It is little consolation as he sees them halfway across the bay before he is barely out of the lagoon. He notices the camera staring down at him from the small archway across its entrance. He grimaces up at it as if someone has told him to say, "cheese," and then wonders what the hell he is doing. He knows it'll be dark by the time he gets there — if he gets there. "At least it's calm," he says to himself.

The adrenaline rush of the gunshot, plus the three beer he's had, have allowed him to forget his aching body for the moment. He knows it's a temporary reprieve and that it will all catch up with him sooner or later. He hopes it's later.

As he paddles, his stomach offers hunger pangs for company. He wonders how that's possible; he ate less than a couple hours ago, and it wasn't Chinese food. The Chinese, Harold believes, are a very clever people. They make food in such a way that you are looking for more just after you think you've stuffed yourself. He does not perceive this conclusion as at all racist. One of the best meals he ever had was a Chinese stir-fry — or was it Vietnamese? No matter, they all come from Asia — that he had ordered accidentally. He couldn't believe you could possibly make a combination of fish bits and broccoli taste good. But it did. He doesn't remember feeling hungry after that meal either. Must have been the fish. He wonders if there's any fish left in the lake. You used to be able to throw a line out anywhere and snag a jack, or even a pickerel if you were lucky. Maybe when he gets to his cabin he'll put together some fishing gear and see what's left. Probably not much between the competing fisheries of sportsmen and the commercial guys throwing their nets across the Mahihkan River. In fact, those two who more or less rescued him the day before were most likely doing just that.

Harold can feel the temperature dropping as the sun sets even though he hasn't actually seen it in several days for all the crappy weather. It occurs to him that he has left his lifejacket back at the marina. It not only is an essential safety device, it provides an extra bit of insulation against the cool and damp. *Way to go, idiot*, he thinks.

A series of vague flashes dance across the horizon. It reminds Harold of those old black and white movies where distant bombing was illuminating the night sky. These are so far away, however, that not even a faint rumble accompanies them. He tries to pick up his pace to work a little more heat into his bones but is only able to sustain it for a short while. He is beyond the point of no return and realizes that he will not make it to shore — any shore — before absolute nightfall. He hopes that the solitary light ahead belongs to the Givens' cabin. On the other hand, he doesn't really care because he's aiming for it no matter what.

A light breeze has picked up and seems to be coming straight into Harold's face. Although he's thankful that it is not crossing his beam, he is struggling to pull the paddle through the water and keep his bow pointed at the light. It never seems to be getting any closer and is the only thing visible on a moonless night. For a short while after the sunset, there was a vague outline that separated land from sky. But that has now disappeared, except when the sky flashes dimly and is now accompanied by dull murmurs.

He considers simply giving up and lying down in the bottom of the canoe and letting the wind drift him back to shore. He'd get there eventually, he knows, and if the wind is truly in his face, he'd end up pretty much where he began — at the Stone's Throw. Which would be worse, this endless struggle to go forward — if he is indeed going forward — or facing whatever mess might be lying behind him?

He thinks of the gunshot and hopes it was merely a warning fired into the air. If it was lethal . . . Harold does not want to go there. It reminds him of Reta and her deliberate blocking of his three-aught-six barrel. Did she really mean him harm? Did she know the potential effect of what she had done? She couldn't have. Could she? This was a woman who thought you put oil in the gas tank when you saw the oil light come on. Who thought you fixed things with a hammer. If that didn't work, you threw them out. She wasn't a bad person. She wasn't a murderer. She was just not very mechanically inclined. He wonders if she's still with that asshole.

Then he feels a drop of water on his face. Is it something the bow has flicked back at him? Or is it rain? Several more drops hit him. His canoe might not make it back merely drifting with the wind. He could drift and bail, but he has nothing to bail *with*. He pulls again with more determination.

The light is getting closer now. Isn't it? You can't tell in the dark. There is no depth perception. Perhaps he is only a couple hundred yards now — the length of two football fields — every stroke a yard or two closer. So, what would that be? Two hundred? Two-fifty? He starts counting.

At stroke ninety-five, a huge fork of lightning splits the wet black sky, and not five seconds later, a stuttering crack of thunder follows. In the brief moment of stark blue light, Harold can see the small skiff bobbing crazily near shore. He knows for certain now that he will soon be safe, warm and dry in Givens' cabin. The thought warms him even though the rain has begun in earnest and the wind now leans against him. But Harold has already passed through fear as he plunges his paddle again and again into the mounting waves, and focuses Zen-like on the light ahead. Another, smaller light appears beneath it. It moves, faltering downward. A flashlight?

"One, twenty-one," dig, pull, "One, twenty-two," dig, pull, "One, twenty-three," dig, pull, "One, twenty . . . "

Another blue burst of illumination reveals a figure apparently getting into the skiff. Then an ear-splitting crack of thunder. This one hits nearby. Are they coming to rescue him? How could they even see him? Just one though, in a red plaid jacket. That would be the Givens woman, Dianne. *What in God's name is she doing?*

25

A Jesus big storm has come crashing down from the northwest. Even though it'll probably blow over in twenty minutes, I feel sorry for the poor sonofabitch in his canoe. I hope he's had the good sense to turn around.

I pick up bits of Davey by hand. I'm surprised by how greasy he is. I mean, they are ashes, but not like wood or coal; they're *human*. The grease would depress him. He was always such a neat freak. I find a small white piece — a tooth, or part of a tooth. It's really small, like a child's. I wonder, do teeth shrink? Or, what if it's not Dave? What if they've mixed the ashes up? I've heard of this happening. We could be carting around the ashes of some six-year old.

I think Dianne might want to know about this — my sister, the stranger, hiding in her room. I would never have guessed in a million years that she and Dave . . . My head just can't go there. I guess technically it's not incest but it still boggles the mind. And then the guitar. All this time, I thought Dave stole it for me. But no. And he's dead. I can't even confront him. What if I found this out while he was alive? What would I have done? What would I say to him? Would I even bother talking? What should I say to Dianne? Nothing. There's nothing to say. It's all been said.

"Are you done?"

Dianne is standing behind me.

"Jesus Christ! You startled me. Done what?"

"Cleaning up."

"Yes, sort of, but I think they might have mixed up the ashes." I pass her what I think is a tooth. "Doesn't this seem a bit small to you?"

"It's a filling," she says. "A ceramic filling. It doesn't burn." She picks up the cookie jar, drops the chip in, and heads for the door.

"Where are you going?"

"Where do you think?"

Before I can answer, she's out the door and into the night, into the storm. I don't know if I should follow her or leave well enough alone. If she wants to dump Dave's ashes into the stormy night, let her. It's more about her and him anyway; apparently I have very little to do with this family.

I don't bother pouring my gin into the teacup. I drink it straight from the bottle, standing at the window watching Dianne heading down towards the lake. Mostly I can just see the path lit in front of her where she points a flashlight. I think she's heading for the boat which I have neglected to pull ashore. I hope it sinks. No, I don't; she'll kill herself if she tries to go out in this. She is my sister, damn it.

I head to the door.

As I slip and stumble my way down to the water, to where I see the small glow of her flashlight, I can hear Dianne pulling at the starter cord. The engine is not catching. I slide the last few feet on my ass and end up knee-deep in the water. The lake water is cooler than the rain that has already completely soaked me. White spume splays across the black rock a dozen or so yards ahead.

"Dianne, this is stupid!" I yell.

"Everything is stupid," she answers, and yanks again on the cord. Twice. She is holding the cookie jar in her arm.

"Let me," I say, climbing aboard. I can tell this is no time for a rational discussion. It's what we came to do so we might as well do it. She moves aside. I have assumed that she has neglected to turn the ignition switch on, or left it in gear, or forgot to prime the engine, but it has all been done. I pull several more times. Still, the motor does not start. And it worked so perfectly earlier in the day.

The rain, which has been coming in torrents, has eased up, lending an odd kind of hush. A weakened flash of lightning signals that it's passing to the south. The rumbles fade.

All at once, from out in the night, we hear a "Hey!" followed by a loud, almost hollow thud, then an erratically frantic splashing. Dianne directs the flashlight towards the sound. From behind the big black rock, a red canoe drifts. It is empty.

"Help! Help!" A voice pleads from behind the rock. The splashing continues. We both know who it is and what has happened.

Dianne hands me the cookie jar; then she takes off her jacket and dives into the water.

26

Harold is grateful that the worst of the intense little squall is over and he can paddle in relative comfort, with the assurance that tonight is not the night he is going to die. He can make out what he thinks is more than one figure around the small light, obviously a flashlight. He can hear the tugs on the starter cord.

A lightning flash from behind him reveals two figures in the boat — the Givenses — and on shore behind them, a large dog. The dog is not looking at the Givenses in the skiff — it is looking beyond them, at him. The dog does not bark as most dogs would.

Harold realizes the dog is a wolf.

"Hey!" he yells.

But in his preoccupation with what he has seen on shore, he does not see the big black rock and strikes it hard, sending him into the dark water while the canoe recoils wildly away.

"Help! Help!" Harold scrambles frantically for the canoe but he is so near exhaustion that he can barely move his arms. However, within seconds, a soft female voice, Dianne's voice, says, "Relax. I've got you." And slowly, Harold is hauled to the big black rock.

When he reaches it, and climbs onto it, she is oddly gone, but he sees Ponytail Guy, Dennis, paddling the skiff with a single oar.

"Dianne!" he cries. "Dianne!" And floating face down is a body. It is halfway between the shore and where Harold now stands on the rock.

"Over there," Harold yells. He watches helplessly as the stupid musician awkwardly pokes the oar in and out of the water trying to make headway towards the body. When he reaches it, he tugs at an arm but cannot pull her weight into the boat.

Harold wonders how this can be, how this is possible — that this woman hauled him to safety and now appears to be dead, floating in the water on the other side of the rock.

"You can stand here. Give me a hand. You can stand here. It's not deep," Dennis pleads. "Help me get her out of the water!"

Harold does so. His belly-flop is the best he can do. It gets him there. He helps load the lifeless body of the beautiful woman into the skiff. He pushes the boat to shore.

"Go get somebody! Anybody!" says the musician.

Harold knows it is at least a four-kilometre walk back to the Stone's Throw, where he will find somebody. Anybody. He doesn't argue. But he does take the flashlight.

He makes it back by dawn. The RCMP are with him — or rather, he is with them. They find Dennis still in the skiff. He is holding Dianne.

27

I know the moment she hits the water that it is not a good thing, that it is not deep enough for diving. As children, we waded ten or twelve yards over submerged boulders lodged in the sand before it was deep enough to swim to the big black rock. But when she rises, slowly, a few yards away, it is clear that she is no longer conscious. And I am powerless to reach her. I poke an oar into the water and try desperately. I call and call her name. But nothing, no response. I am losing her in the dark.

"Over there!" I see Harold, somehow standing on the rock. That fucker is the reason my sister is floating between us. But he's trying to help, pointing.

"I know where she is, damn it, I can't paddle!"

I plunge and push as best I can with my damaged hand. When I reach her, I cannot haul her aboard and beg Harold to help. Which he does, splashing and kicking.

"I can't hardly swim," he says and babbles on about a big dog — a wolf — saving his sorry ass.

"Forget it! Forget it! Just go get help," I tell him. "Take the flashlight!"

Harold stumbles off.

I am now sitting with my sister, Dianne, and my brother Davey in a small boat. We are floating. The three of us. Flying around the room.

"Thank you, Denny. How did you get so strong? I think I am dead. I think there are angels, and they are so shiny, I can't see their faces. They make buzzing sounds. I don't remember breathing. I just remember . . . flying," says Dianne.

"You're floating now," I say. "I always thought I'd die before you, Dianne. I deserve to die before you. Why is it the bums live and the good people die? We spend a couple nights together in twenty-five years and we find more out about each other than we ever knew, and what do you do? You go and do this — you die on me. What the hell kind of thing is that? I can't tell what you mean to me — it's too . . . we don't have language for that kind of thing. We have songs."

"I'm sorry about the guitar."

"I don't think apologies work, *post-mortem*."

"I'm not dead yet. I'm just about dead, but not quite. I can hear everything you're saying."

"I didn't say anything."

"Then I can hear you thinking. Don't think so loud."

"I don't know how to control the volume, Dianne."

"Just turn the knob."

"The knob?"

"All those things you want to say to people before they die? Well, now's your chance."

"I don't know where to start . . . I love you."

"That was a good place . . . I love you too."

"I'm sorry for all the lies I told you."

"Why?"

"Well, because they weren't the truth. I was hiding. Behind the lies."

"You can hide behind the truth too, Denny. We all hide behind something. And now you know."

"And now I know. Yeah. I'm sorry, Dianne. I'm sorry for all this."

"Don't be."

"I'm not. I just said it because . . . I don't know why. I just say things. It doesn't explain much."

"No, it doesn't."

"It doesn't explain why I am the way I am."

"It doesn't have to."

"If I could only have found some kind of movement — like politics or Christ — maybe I could be a whole person."

"Don't bullshit me now, Den."

"No, of course not. Now is not the time . . . "

"No,"

"You're quite the person, Dianne. I'm going to miss you. Do you have anything to say to me?"

"No."

"Oh."

"I suppose I should ask the question, though."

"What?"

"Will you forgive me?"

I linger here a bit while the post-storm waves gently lap the skiff shoreward. We'll be nudging it soon.

"No," I say. "You haven't done anything wrong. This is actually backward; I should be asking your forgiveness."

"I forgive you."

"Thank you. Are we even?"

"Take care of Kirsten."

"Oh, right."

"And Mom."

"I'll do the best I can."

"That's not good enough."

"It's all I can do."

"I guess that's it, then."

"We should sign off, or whatever."

"I guess so."

"Goodbye, Dianne."

"Goodbye Dennis."

"Oh, you want to know what?"

"What?"

"This is the best talk we've ever had."

Behind the cabin, I can see red and blue flashing lights.

I watch the leaves turn, and cross down from "the Cove", now reclaimed in shoots of black poplar and stinging nettles, the place where Harold's cabin once stood. I drink at water's edge where thin crystal ice plates have begun to form next to a red canoe overturned on the bank. Nearby, blue smoke rises from the flue to a white trapper's tent. Harold's hands are blackened from bucking the charcoal-coated pine he now splits with his axe.

Harold thinks I am a dog. "Here boy," he says. He throws fish scraps to me. I inspect them to be polite, but leave them for Raven. Her soul is hungrier than mine.

He talks to me, but not in words. He talks about love. I see it on how he strikes the wood, gathers the split pieces, and stacks them in careful rows. He talks about hope. I see it in how he gathers water from the near shore, cooks, and sharpens his tools. He talks about loneliness. I see it in how his gaze strikes the horizon when the faint sound of a boat motor reaches his ear.

This day his gaze lingers. A small boat appears in the cove. In it is Denny and a young woman. Kirsten.

I saunter into the brush. Become invisible.

Denny has lost weight and looks younger. He and Kirsten unload several boxes and containers of fuel. A set of keys for their cabin in case they should need it. They are going on a quest to find someone, they say.

Jimmy Matheson. I hope they find him.

They leave.

Quiet rolls out after them till only night is left.

Soon, a thick white carpet of snow will lie over the lake. Deer will stay close to shore. Bear will sleep. Only Raven and I will cross it, mute.

But Raven will sometimes laugh. She cannot help herself. She is my sister.

I will sometimes sing.

R.P. MacIntyre is best known for his award-winning young adult fiction. He has also written for television, radio, and the stage, and has edited and compiled over thirty-five anthologies of YA fiction, one of which won the Canadian Librarian Association's Book of the Year in 1997. *Mahihkan Lake* is his seventh book and his first adult novel.